AMONRA:

God of Kings, King of Gods

Horus Michael

AMONRA:

God of Kings, King of Gods

Horus Michael

AMONRA: God of Kings, King of Gods

This book was printed in the U.S.A.

First Edition © 2015 MC

www.amazon.com/author/horusmichael

Genre: Action & Adventure, Fantasy, Fiction.

(**6x9**) Hieroglyph Font by **Inscribe**.

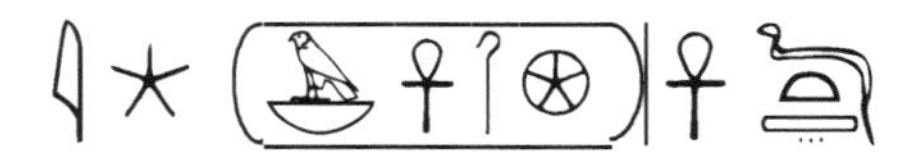

For Lynn Bellair; Aunt Sandra and Cousin Jenni (2015):

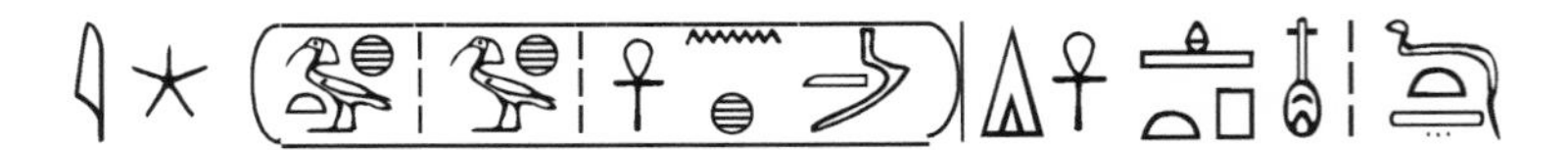

Chapter 1:

Crossed scepters only meant one concept in the Ancient Egyptian mindset: DEATH. You can see this in dead insects, with their arms crossed against their chest. No, there was no "curse" of the Pharaohs - You fool, you are staring right at it, all the time! Every bodily sign was a message, a pictograph, a secret handshake, a gesture of an old Secret Society of Priests. X meant DEATH, so every time you glance at the crossed-scepters of some Golden Pharaoh, he is *cursing you*, showing the Next World his power and authority which outshines the grave. Among us there was one who had the power to regenerate cells and give back life. He was immortal, for most purposes though, he could return to life, in a new and improved form. What was his name? Allusive... It was...

"MICHAEL!" Words came to my mind, swimming with ideas, brimming in brilliance like flower petals dipped in coffee... Oh, Coffee, with a hint of mint? Where was I? Lost in a field of ideas, I typed whatever came to me. The shadowy High Priest of AmonRa, the gregarious Pharaoh, the stubborn Vizier and a Mistress with her enigmatic smile...

"Michael, can you hear me?" The voice was vaguely familiar, though the outside heat clocked over 90F this splendid afternoon in our tri-level cabin over in Washington State. My laptop computer hastily recorded my novel in between sips of Maui Blend and the banging of one window down below, the one with a female voice trying to gain my attention. One more paragraph and my chapter would be complete. One last punctuation mark: Done. Hit Enter, and Save.

I leaned back in my padded leather swivel chair, my eyeglasses with transition lenses resting comfortably on my Italian nose. My eyes closed for one instance of intellectual gratification... Then it hit me.

"Michael if you don't open this door, I'm calling Roger!" interrupted the serene silence of defeating Writer's Block. The voice was my sister, Carmine. Roger was her BFF, a Black Belt in Aikido, and a damn good Cook.

I sighed slightly. Regaining my consciousness, I adjusted my bow-tie, combed my slick-black hair with a common instrument, and slammed my laptop until it gently met its bottom cover. Then I ran downstairs to greet Carmine. The door was almost within reach.

"Ah, Carmine! Sweet as ever. Can I interest you in some Espresso?" I asked through the wire mesh after unlocking its double-bolt and opening the front door.

Carmine met my eyes with a smile. Then I turned to greet her upraised hand, the one holding my rental agreement. I was 2 weeks late in recurring payments. Damn, I forgot about that one.

"Okay. Well, you know Carmine, I haven't had decent work in a few months..." I started. "Doesn't Roger have financial issues?"

She inserted the accompanying letter in between the rental agreement and my face. Something halfway down met me in bewilderment.

"Ah! You were accepted to Williamford University? Congratulations! I know how much that meant to you, and well... Roger," I said sheepishly. Williamford was only the best Ivy League College in the lower 49 States. What was her subject of study? Paraphysics? Organic Informatics? Certainly not Junior Literature!

"Actually I am majoring in Ancient Astronomy. What? It's a good subject. There are jobs for it, over in...China," Carmine replied between sips of Maui Blend Coffee.

"We're not outsourcing Ancient Astronomers to China. Haven't you read the newspapers? Chinese nuclear technology is making Russian leaders nervous, you know, the Third Superpower and all..." I said while fixing an egg sandwich in the kitchen. Damn, I'm out of Mayonnaise.

"Michael? How can you live without decent food? I see you up there working on some Ian Green Tome, or some possible Pulitzer Prize for Extravagance. Now you're fixing a sandwich without Mayo? Who does your cooking - the Automaton from Xani-X?" Xani-X was not just the best Sci-Fi flick to grace the Silver Screen; it was also highly influential over in Food Village Superstores. My substitution with Mustard extorted a slight chuckle from her direction.

The kitchen was adjacent to the front door by a meter of fine marble tiles. Outside were 2 miles of woodland, thick evergreen pine trees, a swimming pool, a General Store, and the town Church. The dry air was waiting for a wildfire to burst open. A thick trench protected our home's perimeter for the most part.

"I was working on this book, a historical-fantasy one about the Egyptian God AmonRa - you know, Wind and Sunlight combined and personified. It's like Roger, sort of..." I said after refilling my porcelain cup with Maui Blend Coffee.

"Oh, Roger is not full of hot air!" Carmine snapped.

"Did I say hot? Did I say hot?" I defended.

"You said, you implied... Well, I forgive you," Carmine said. "It's good Coffee, by the way. I can't for the love of me see how you can afford it on your paycheck."

"AmonRa, the God of Kings, the King of Gods - he was a King after all, you know. He's royalty," I admired for a second.

"Isn't he a God of War? Or Fertility?" Carmine related.

"There are many uses, some usurped from others," I said. "My book does none of those things. For that, I need research! Carmine, fetch Roger's vacation photos from his last trip to Egypt for me. I am sure it's still in storage."

"Why Egypt?" She asked me silently, her voice hiding an unknown guilt. "Why the mystery?"

"Egypt has fascinated me for eons. They had everything - technology, organized society, slave labor - if you discount the recent discoveries of budding Egyptologists looking for fame - then something happened and they all disappeared. Wiped from History, so where did they all go?" I asked her.

"Maybe they left in Space Ships? Or mingled with other cultures?" Carmine mocked my research.

"Or, perhaps they left for the New World and influenced the Aztecs and Mayans? Ideas and technology survive wipeouts. The Chinese didn't just happen to have Ushabtis for the First Emperor's Afterlife Army, or models of food and drink under the Ming Dynasty for no reason. Mayan priests with Jaguar skins versus Egyptian priests with Leopard skins; what are the parallels?" I spoke at length.

"You forgot Hawaii and Ancient Polynesia," Carmine smiled.

"Exactly. Hawaiian royalty possessed the power of the Gods in their blood, in their bones... A Transcultural enterprise of thousands of years!" I elated in excitement. Carmine lifted her head with her hands below the chin, propped up by her elbows on the kitchen table. Her Coffee cup was empty, so I returned to the stove to refill it.

"I just love Lucky Tikis. Did you know they stopped producing Tikis from lava rock? Someone said it was unlucky. It's not like the stone itself is unlucky," Carmine's eyes met the back wall as she sipped Maui Blend for a few minutes.

"The Stone... That's it!" I said quickly.

"What?" She asked.

"The Stone, don't you see? It has *energy* in it. The energy acts on people's will or imagination, thus producing an effect related to their thoughts! Carmine, you're *brilliant!"* I exclaimed.

"I am? But I haven't started College yet," She said quietly.

I ran upstairs, into the Guest room. I frantically searched my closet for Hawaiian Lava rocks legally purchased from a decade ago, and the book about Energy Vortexes.

"Aha! I found some!" I shouted against the back wall. I gathered the items and brought them downstairs into the Living room. Carmine followed me there.

"Michael, you're not going to be making a mountain out of mashed potatoes or anything, right?" Carmine cautioned.

I placed one Hawaiian Lava rock stone on the table, with an apparatus of Egyptian ritual focused on the rock using the Skylight above us. I waited for the right moment, and then I used the apparatus to send focused sunlight onto the Lava rock while cutting it with a diamond ring I was wearing. A few seconds passed and we both heard a popping noise. The Lava rock split open. Inside was a crystallized group of strange diamonds with illumination. I held the rock in my free hand, and then I thought about water, more specifically rain.

"Michael? I hear something outside," Carmine looked to the back window and sure enough there was rain.

I opened my eyes. Then I looked towards the Lava rock.

"The Ancient Egyptians gave their Philosopher Stones to the Polynesians?" I asked in astonishment. The Philosopher Stones were a creation of Alchemy, first devised in the Middle Ages to produce gold from base metals. The Stones themselves contained great mystery. Each Stone was mentally controlled by willed ideas, like a computer that read one's thoughts and produced or created the object of thought. This was once property of the Pharaohs or the High Priests of AmonRa?

"So does that mean they're lucky?" Carmine asked while sipping Coffee.

"I'm going to have to test this," I replied. "Normal Lava rock doesn't just have diamonds in base basalt. But, apply focused sunlight to it and you have something else."

"Is it a Laser?" Carmine asked.

"Perhaps. Sunlight has an effect," I said. I picked up one severed rock and turned it in my hands while shining sunlight there. Then the Sun moved. I glanced at my watch. It read: 3:30pm. The rain stopped a few minutes afterwards.

An hour later I assembled this makeshift Hawaiian Tiki statue on a rock altar in the back yard. I added a plastic flower lei, two whole coconuts, and Lava rock on the base. Reading from a Native Hawaiian Magic book I performed a water ceremony over the next ten minutes. That was done after a moment, so I switched to an Egyptian solar incantation. The ground started to tremble.

"Earthquake! Move!" Carmine yelled. The ground burst open right in front of us, knocking both of us to the surface.

"Michael? Why would an Egyptian Amulet be found in Northern Washington State?" Carmine asked as we crawled to a stand.

"An Amulet?" I asked her. She pointed to the ground.

Sure enough a small find was visible. Glowing with an eerie emanation of revolving lights, an amulet appeared right below the Lava rock. The item was a *Criosphinx* head with a loop near the horns. Its construction seemed to me of fine gold with semi-precious stone inlay mixed with Tiki diamonds. I reached down and picked it up, analyzing it before wearing it.

"I wonder what this does?" I asked the amulet. The item was not as heavy as first suggested.

"Well if it's thought controlled, do you just hold it and think of something?" Carmine thought aloud.

"That's an idea, Carmine. Close your eyes, please," I said. She obeyed.

I held the precarious item clasped in my right fist, held in place around my neck with its chain link necklace. I thought about Ancient Egypt, and about AmonRa. My next thought was not as well-planned.

I felt this pulsating energy take over my appearance. My skin became bronzed, my attire transformed into Late 19th Dynasty white linen and a golden corselet with beaded collar, and my hair had this flat, Queen Nefertiti crown on it. When I opened my eyes, I saw my reflection in the rippling swimming pool surface.

"Michael? You look like King Ramses from the *10 Commandments* film. You should take a look," Carmine related.

"All this from Hawaiian Lava rock, an Egyptian focus laser, and a little sunlight... Now I am dressed like a god," I said to my reflection.

When I released my grip on the amulet, my clothing returned to normal, as did my skin. "Hmm..."

Chapter 2:

The next day I stopped work on my novel. I had other - *ideas* - worth exploring. There was this storm approaching Washington State from the West - a leftover from a Hurricane in Hawaii. We were driving, Roger was actually. I was giving directions to the GPS computer voice. Carmine was seated behind us in her friend's sedan. My amulet was secretly hidden behind my double-breasted suit. Roger wanted to show me his work in the City. I tagged along just to escape the imprisonment of the Cabin.

"So, Michael, I hear you're quite the novelist," Roger broke the silence.

"Yes. You're an excellent driver, too," I replied. "How is the Stock Market these days?"

Roger was a Stock Broker. It was a nine-to-five job with great benefits and some room to advance. We were here at 6am, just in time to greet his boss, a row of computers, and the café for some belated Caffeine. The work was hectic to say the least. All this rushing around, getting quotes, it seemed like he'd die of a heart attack if he stopped to brush his teeth. No, just the gold ones in front, all the others had crowns.

An hour in and we had a Bull Market. That was until the news broke: "Breaking News! Chinese Markets crashed after the Premier said he was not allowing nuclear inspectors inside the Reactor. Apparently the Reactor is leaking... More information at eleven..." A minute later, there was a massive sell-off. The Dow Jones dropped 200 points in twenty seconds. I had to do something. Then it occurred to me.

I reached into my jacket and grasped the Amulet when no one was watching. My skin started to bronze.

"No... not here, too embarrassing," I said to myself. I entered a small bathroom and locked myself in it. Everyone else was scurrying about anyway. No one noticed me. I shut my eyes for 5 seconds, and then opened them.

"Whoa! It couldn't be, could it? I look just like AmonRa!" I said to my reflection in the chrome bathroom mirror. "Think. Oh of course, AmonRa was a god of the poor, of prosperity. Think about money, lots of it."

"Michael? Are you okay?" Carmine rattled at the door.

"Just a minute, I'm washing my face," I lied. A moment later I heard cheers from the office. The NYSE just gained 500 points in the positive direction. There was an instant Bull Market.

The amulet glowed until I released my grip. I slowly returned to normalcy. My face no longer appeared bronzed, except for a slight tan around my eyeglasses.

"Hey, Michael! Good News from New York," Carmine related.

I opened the door. Carmine greeted me warmly. I smiled slightly.

Roger was seated in his chair, a stack of papers teetering aside his laptop computer. His coffee cup glistened with black coffee as two sugar cubes fell into place. He twiddled a pair of #2 pencils between his fingers.

"So Michael, when did you get a tan?" Roger asked about my eyeglasses aura. The bronzing effect doesn't exactly go away.

I smiled slightly.

"Roger! Get back in the ring. We have a client whose buying up Macrosoft stocks at $2 each," his boss informed him.

Roger looked at me, twice, and then stood up and returned to the rat race of stock buying. It was like this all day. When the

NYSE closed to a ringing bell, Roger was exhausted. I stood by the window, staring at the incoming rain storm. Carmine was polishing her fingernails and blowing to cool the paint. A crack of thunder ended the moment. I knew what I had to do. And this wasn't going to be easy either.

Chapter 3:

An archaic painting of the Egyptian Ocean God Nunu supporting Ra's boat into the sky rested on a cluttered shelf in some Museum of Egyptology in downtown Seattle. We drove all this way to confirm my suspicions. There was something about that Amulet, and it wasn't right. Who did it belong to? Where did it come from? Why was it made?

"Over here is an 18th Dynasty Map of plundered tombs written by a tomb robber by the name Djed-Ka-Nefer. In the description he mentions two things - a gold-plated bronze dagger, and an amulet of *the God* AmonRa," the Curator introduced the collection to a small group of tourists.

"Did he say what the amulet looked like? Was it gold or silver?" asked Carmine. She was dressed in a fashionable mini-skirt with red shoes, with a short matching red shirt.

"This papyrus does not specify exactly what the amulet was manufactured from, but there is this Magic Spell associated with it," the Curator said. "It will give the bearer the powers of the god AmonRa."

"Whose tomb was it?" I interrupted.

"Oh... Some High Priest or Divine Scribe," the Curator replied.

A man watched us from the restroom area. He took a few snapshots of us with his Pear-2 Cell Phone. Then he quickly departed.

"...The bearer having the powers of the god will appear immortal. He can fly, repel arrows, affect the weather, transform rocks into gold nuggets, and anything the human mind can imagine," he said. "Anything. Now does that sound like a Myth, or some Kentucky Jane novel?"

"Hold on," I stopped. The man in the back room returned. This time his gloved hands held a Glock handgun with silencer, pointing in our direction.

I instinctively reached into my jacket, and grabbed the amulet. Carmine saw the man, and dove for cover behind an Information Kiosk. The man fired two rounds, one hitting the Curator's papyrus. The man fired again. I had to do something. So I did.

"Michael! Your face, your skin... And that costume? What's going on?" Carmine asked while crouching on the thinly carpeted Museum floor.

"My *God*... You, you *have* the amulet?" the Curator said.

I appeared in the room wearing Egyptian armor - a *Khepesh* helm of blue leather, an iron and gold scaled cuirass, white linen kilt with an unknown metal for leg armor, and leather-wrapped sandals. Halloween wasn't for another 3 months. The man fired in my direction. So I lifted up one arm, and the bullets fell back like water droplets. I thought for a moment. The ground underneath the man transformed into snakes that wrapped about his legs, holding him there.

The man was overcome with fear, so I tackled him to the tiled floor of the Museum Café. I asked him who he is. He told me everything.

"I am a Knight of the Golden Cross. The Amulet was stolen from our organization long ago during the Crusades in the Holy Land, and stolen again recently. We believe the thief hid it someplace in Washington State, according to our GPS tracking on a bug hidden in the Amulet's chain. That was 40 weeks ago. Now *you* have it," the man replied.

"Why did you *fire* on us?" I demanded.

"I thought you were the thief! Honestly, I had *no idea* you would actually be using it.

Only the *Chosen One* has the ability to wield its power correctly," he said. "Its power is mentally controlled."

"What about Lava rock?" Carmine asked him. "We discovered..."

"No. Whoever is in close proximity to the amulet will access its powers. Lava rocks have no power," the man said. "Nice tan, by the way."

"Thanks. Tell me more about the Golden Cross," I asked him.

"We... We are the protectors of the Lost Shrine of AmonRa. Our people have Genealogical heirs from AmonRa's priesthood in the last millennia. We swore an oath to protect the Shrine, and guard its amulet. Now *you* have it," he said.

"All right, suppose I believe this and you're correct. What's next?" I asked him. His face was suddenly overcome with hesitation.

"There is one problem... The *Amulet of Apophis* was also stolen recently. We have no way of knowing its location," the man said in dread.

"Apophis? The Asteroid Apophis?" I asked him.

"No... The sworn enemy of AmonRa was the *Dragon* Apophis. While AmonRa was light, Apophis was darkness. Where AmonRa is Good, Apophis was Evil. They are polar opposites, like *Yin and Yang*," he said.

"So who is wearing the Amulet of Apophis?" Carmine asked.

"Legend has it only a bearer of the *opposite gender* can wield its power. So as your friend has the Amulet of AmonRa, its opposite must be a *woman*..." the man said in slurred speech.

"Well I'm not wearing it. It's not even my style," Carmine grinned.

A dark shadow appeared through the Museum skylight above. The Knight saw this and shivered uncontrollably. With his whole body shaking, he managed to point towards the shape above us before he passed out.

The shadow on the floor resembled a large tentacle or tail of some kind. A moment later the Sun reappeared. As we remained focused on the shadow, the Knight regained consciousness and grasped my left forearm, whispering something into my ear. The day wasn't over yet.

Chapter 4:

We drove to a local pub. I ordered a round of Dark Ale with potato chips. The Knight accompanied us - we still data-mined his brain for information. Carmine searched the pub for colorful postcards and tourist junk in the lobby. The darkness of the pub changed my transition lenses back to clear. As my eyes grew accustomed to the light, I noticed this athletic brunette wearing a red frock or body sheath with red stiletto pumps seated four bar stools to my right. Her turquoise eyes fired back and reflected off her Martini's glass. I introduced myself.

"Yes, I am a writer. Oh? Mostly Historical-Fantasy," I replied. The girl said she studied mixed-Martial arts, with a Minor in Ancient History. Her name was *Si-Hithor*, but in Ancient Egyptian transcription the name was Sat-Hathor, as in a daughter of the *Goddess of Love*. I don't believe her name was native to her, probably more like a *Nom de Plume*?

"My mother named me that, after a childhood experience rendered me partly paralyzed on my left side. We had been visiting the *Osirion* in Abydos, Egypt that week. The surrounding rocks seemed unusually slippery as I was climbing them. But you know - tourists should not climb rocks?" She laughed. "Anyway, I was bitten by a rare spider; its toxins paralyzed me for an hour. Mom went to get help, and I fell into a pool while searching for the bug. Rumors said the Osirion had *healing powers* in its waters. Naturally I didn't believe in local superstition... I was submerged for a few seconds, and Mom pulled me out. Then I noticed I was cured. So Mom called me *Si-Hithor* and the name stuck ever since."

"Do you mind my asking about your former name?" I asked her.

"Jill. Jill Carson," she smiled. "And yours?"

"Yes... I'm Michael--," I stopped. A dark cloud blocked the sunlight behind the pub windows behind her. A shadowy reptilian shape was thrashing about in the sky. Jill's mouth dropped from the reflection in my eyeglasses. She turned about face.

"Oh my F—ing God," she gasped.

"Carmine! It's time to go," I announced.

We exited the pub momentarily before a fireball struck it, blowing out all the windows. More fireballs hit the earth from above. The sunlight though brilliant left us in the shadow of this long-tailed monster above, the one with hundreds of silvery spikes and one very large, fanged, fire-spewing mouth. Carmine glanced towards me, and then gestured for my absence.

I ran around to the back of the pub and grabbed the Amulet of AmonRa tightly. In seconds my skin was bronzed, and my clothes became the vestment of the Great God once again. Jill searched for me frantically before seeing this golden blur fly into the air.

The normally clear sky was rife with thunderclouds and dangerous lightning, encircling the Beast. Its tail extended over a mile in length, with strong limbs and iron talons in each grip. Above its mouth had this Oriental Moustache of two curvy whiskers opposite its flared nostrils. Almost the sound of a sonic boom was the voice of the Beast.

"AmonRa, *my brother*, finally you have arrived," the Beast spoke. "Bow *before* Apophis!"

"*Who are you?* Where is the Amulet of Apophis?" I demanded.

"The Amulet? The Amulet is ... in safe keeping. I am Apophis, the Dragon, *Archenemy* of the Lord of Light, AmonRa! Where is *your* amulet?" said the Dragon.

With that said, I directed a *tornado* towards the center of the Dragon's personal sphere. Apophis could not deflect this one. Despite lightning and golf-ball sized hailstorms, the tornado sucked up everything in its midst, including a small Amulet in the shape of a serpent. A person was seen falling to its death afterwards, wearing dark clothing. I descended to the ground and picked up the amulet, and then I turned to leave. Carmine turned around to distract Jill so I could hide in the deserted pub.

"Where, *where* did Michael go?" Jill Carson asked while looking about. "Oh, there you are!" she grinned as I appeared in the broken glass of the pub.

"Michael, you missed all the action. AmonRa was here again," Carmine lied. "That was one *big* lizard."

The Knight of the Golden Cross appeared dazed and confused. "Did you obtain the *cursed* Amulet?" he asked me.

"Here, keep it safe," I handed the Amulet of Apophis to him.

"But who wielded it?" the Knight asked me as we approached the corpse a half-mile away. The road contained a figure in all-black clothing, including a hood and face mask. I knelt to the pavement. Peeling the mask away revealed a blond-haired woman with a *tattoo* of a Serpent eating a crucifix *on her neck*.

"What is this? It's the insignia of the *Servitude of the Dragon Empress*? I thought they had been extinct!" the Knight elated.

"Who?" I asked politely.

"It's a *Secret Society* of Dragon-mancers who lived in the 14th Century. They manufactured *Amulets of Apophis*, like the one you recovered. The only problem was we thought they all died out during the Black Plague and the Great Purge era." The Knight covered up the face of the corpse with part of its cloak. "The *stolen* Amulet of Apophis was just one of many."

"There's more than *one* of them?" I asked in disbelief.

"Yes, and they're all female. In Italy we call them the *Dark Harem*. You probably require my knowledge of how to *use* the Amulet of AmonRa properly?" the Knight said.

Carmine smiled at me. “Don’t quit your day job, Mike.”

Chapter 5:

One week passed by. Carmine and I took a vacation to Egypt with the Knight's help. He escorted us to a medium size house in Eastern Alexandria. The Shrine to AmonRa existed in the cellar. One needed special access to reach it.

"The Catacombs extends from here," the Knight remarked. "But the Shrine is hidden below this manhole cover. There, the ladder leads to a grotto where the Shrine is kept."

We descended the ladder into a room alight with hundreds of votive candles made from beeswax. Stained glass decorated the interior with light reflected from above. The Shrine resembled an inverted boat. I asked him why.

"The later people who visited and preserved the Shrine were Coptic Christians. They built churches in the shape of upside-down boats. Ahead is the Shrine," the Knight said.

Chanting in some archaic *lingua franca* echoed from wooden pews in the next room. Golden Crosses protected the walls from *evil spirits* while cisterns full of sacred water aligned the halls. Dominating the sanctuary stood this solid gold statue of AmonRa with inlays of Abalone shell, lapis lazuli, and Emeralds mined in Egypt during the age of the Ptolemy Pharaohs.

"He even has Emerald eyes," Carmine related.

A dozen Priests dressed in Green Cloaks met us in the Sanctuary. Two of them cast burnt Frankincense from chained steel vessels. A third was polishing the Statue itself with an old silk rag. At the base of the Statue were baskets of fresh fruit and vegetable offerings. Prayer scrolls seemed to be stuffed into the wine racks along one wall, some bearing ancient Papyri and parchment. The air was warm despite natural air conditioning coming from the Catacombs to the south.

A Priest noticed the Amulet of AmonRa resting on my chest on its chain link necklace. He turned it about in his hands, and then remarked that the GPS receiver was still in place. It was a small stainless-steel Scarab attached as a spacer bead. The Priest rose up some praise for about a minute, and the others danced a little jig to the sound of a rattle.

"So what's going on, Sir Knight?" I asked the Knight by tugging on his cloak.

"The Commune is deciding on your new appointment as Guardian of the Shrine," he said to me. "They seem to like the idea."

"Whoa - I'm not staying here," I stopped.

"You are the *Chosen One.* Relax, it's not like we didn't know. Observe the story of the Prophecy on our video," the Knight said as he switched on a video system. Two view-screen monitors popped into place from behind stained glass windows.

The video lasted about an hour and was directed by a young *Omar Sharif.* A Scribe encounters the Amulet of AmonRa via an earthquake, challenges a follower of Apophis, and becomes AmonRa's Image on the Earth as the *Chosen One.* This *Chosen One* must battle the followers of Apophis and win, enabling peace and justice to once again maintain the realm of the living. The Scribe's facial features looked like my driver's license but with auburn hair.

"Ha, my hair is actually *black,*" I said at length.

"No Mike, actually you were *born* with reddish-brown hair. Mom said you were born with this incurable color-changing virus. I thought she told you that?" Carmine suggested.

"Really?" I asked. "My Driver License is public domain - *anyone* could acquire it. There are *websites* for that."

"Michael? This Video was produced *before* your birth," a Priest commented.

I swallowed hard.

The evening winds forced the hotel to close its windows early to avoid Dust Storms in the forecast. I was in the Hotel's outdoor bar, sipping a non-alcoholic beverage, wearing white slacks and leather slippers. My blue collared shirt lay unbuttoned from the third row down. Carmine finished one lap in the Hotel pool before dripping past me to the Jacuzzi. Seven women jumped into the pool, and played *Marco Polo* for an hour.

I held the Amulet of AmonRa in my ringed hands, rotating it in the given sunlight, admiring its craftsmanship. The *Criosphinx* head displayed two curved ram horns terminating in carved diamonds, and golden lettering of Ancient Hieroglyphs of the name *AmonRa, Lord of Light*, etched into the base. The reverse was written in Hieratic Script; a Magic Spell to activate the device - which basically read "*Wear this to awaken AmonRa.*"

My cellular phone rang a few ringtones. I answered the third one. Si-Hithor wanted to ask me out to dinner in Washington State. No one told her about my recent sabbatical.

The Knight had given me a book about the powers of the Amulet, which I read by poolside. One of the abilities was teleportation, meaning I could think of a location and a False Door would appear on any solid wall with which I could pass through. Another was Invisibility, and a third one could influence the Seasons - *Climate Change in a bottle*, so to speak. The amulet itself was fashioned from the *Egyptian Philosopher's Stone*, as I initially thought. Sadly, I was wrong about the Lava rocks, *at least for now.*

Chapter 6:

Two hours later, I had just left the swimming pool area and was walking in the hotel towards the escalators. Someone on the top level flashed a device in my direction, possibly a camera. This reminded me of the Knight initially. So I ran up the escalator, avoiding the other people riding it. Upon reaching the top level, I noticed a leg move and felt a kick attack my right face, knocking me down. This blond girl was standing there, with a Serpent amulet around her neck. The woman started to trample me with her leather-heeled Italian pumps, but when her foot was almost touching my larynx I managed to grasp the Amulet of AmonRa with a free hand. I thought about Wind, since AmonRa is a God of Air. Suddenly the woman lost her balance as this forceful gust of wind pushed her down the escalators. I managed to crawl to a stand in time to see her hit the ground, get up, and run away. I approached the side of the escalators and sat on it, sliding all the way down to ground level. The woman saw me and darted into the Computer Arcade room. I followed her.

Numerous computer sounds, music and noises made it close to impossible to hear anything else. I noticed some classic games - Donkey Kong, Pac-Man, and Outrun - were stationed in the back of the room nearest a crossbow arcade game. Two brass-token exchange machines mirrored the entrance. A clearing was in the room's center. The blond woman stood there as if waiting for me. She selected a Martial Arts pose.

"You can at least tell me who you are," I started. "Are you an agent of Apophis?"

She ran towards me, and Cartwheeled a kick in my direction, then pushed off the ground with her hands and landed both feet aside my shoulders, knocking me down. Her bare legs wrapped about my neck in some Jujitsu hold, almost strangling me. I inched my hands to the Amulet, and then realized that was unnecessary for thought-control. So I imagined the ceiling turning into ice. Then I heard something above crack, like when a drink is poured into an ice-filled glass. The woman looked upwards, and screamed as the ceiling collapsed onto her. Her legs moved away from my body, so I could crawl to a stand. She stood up and grimaced angrily. Then her hands posed in a tiger claw formation. She wasn't done yet.

Four blows followed, one penetrated my defensive stance and ripped off my eyeglasses. This was countered by two blocks. She flipped backwards and kicked my head with a sideways movement. I saw my opportunity and tripped her with my leather slipper, which fell off. I then grabbed both of her arms and pulled her back to my chest. She motioned a high kick upwards, like a cheerleader. As I was deflecting it, she took my arm and flipped my body over her in a Judo move. Then she started to trample my face with her Italian pumps, just barely missing my nose. I grabbed her foot, twisted it, and knocked her down, and then wrestled her to the carpet - my head above hers. She was breathing heavily with this look of anger on her face. I grinned slightly, then she spat into my eyes.

"You need to tell me everything," I said to the woman.

She said something in broken Italian, and then slapped my face with her free left hand before grasping her Amulet of Apophis. A few moments later a mysterious fog enveloped her body. She smiled as her body teleported away from me, leaving me in a push-up position on the carpet.

I stood up. In examining the room I found something she left behind. It was a business card of some sort. No address was visible, only a phone number and a name. The name was in Italian. I returned to my hotel room a few minutes later.

As I opened the door, I called out for Carmine. Then I noticed something. The room was ransacked. Books were lying on the carpet, clothing was in disarray, furniture was moved, and my luggage was obviously disturbed. I heard the sound of water running. So I checked the bathroom. It was locked.

"Carmine, are you in there?" I knocked on the door. Not hearing a reply, I inserted a credit card in between the lock and the doorframe until it unlocked. The shower curtain was closed. I pulled it back.

"CARMINE!" I yelled. She was lying on the bottom of the shower, unconscious despite slash wounds on her face, shoulder and arms. I checked her vitals - she was still alive. I flipped out my cell phone and called the Front Desk. An Emergency crew was there in minutes.

An hour later in the local hospital I waited impatiently in a small room filled with people. The doors opened. A nurse wearing a light blue face mask with matching clothing approached me and ushered me inside.

"How is she?" I inquired.

"She is stable. The Doctor prescribed pain medicine and tranquilizers. Her wounds are not life-threatening. And her breathing was somewhat erratic, so she is using a breathing tube until we can stabilize it. Does she have Medical Insurance?" the Nurse said.

"Yes. In the States she does," I replied.

"Good then," she said. "I recommend a few days of treatment before being released."

"Can I see her?" I implored.

"I will check first," the Nurse replied. "Yes. You can go in."

I entered a room separated by walls of blue cloth. Carmine was sleeping, with clear plastic breathing tubes supplying her with Oxygen. Her wounds had been mended, with some stitches and cloth bandages. I noticed her speckled hospital gown and brushed brown hair. Someone had left behind a bouquet of fresh roses on a night stand, possibly from a neighboring booth. The heartbeat device was bouncing about in regular beats. I took one of her hands and held it for a minute, it was still warm.

On closer examination of the roses' bouquet I saw this one object resting on the table. It was a Golden Cross.

Chapter 7:

Four days later, Carmine was released from the hospital. In that time, I contacted the Knights of the Golden Cross in the Shrine of AmonRa, in Alexandria. They referred me to visit the Golden Cross's spiritual leader, Aqen. Aqen lived simply in this Monastery near Sinai Peninsula. Occupying a few acres of Monastic property, Aqen told me his Knights already knew of the incursion of Apophis agents in Egypt and that one Knight visited Carmine in the hospital. He gave me the address of a Knight to contact. So I did. The only problem was he lives on Cyprus Island, to the north of Egypt. We boarded a plane there once Carmine was fit to travel.

The twin-engine Cessna airplane circled twice and then landed on a private airstrip on Cyprus. This was a night flight. The sprawling Castle wasn't visible from the air. A small black SUV Limousine met us on the ground as we walked from the Terminal. The driver opened a door and this man dressed in a green & yellow, Turkish Military uniform introduced us.

"Sir Michael? Greetings, I am Sir Lucas of the Golden Cross. Welcome to Cyprus," he said smiling.

We rode the Limousine up this winding rocky road for about 30 minutes. I was thankful I didn't have Motion Sickness. The road led to four miles of farmland and vineyards, said to be owned by the organization. Finally we reached our destination - a mile of tall hedges hid a large stone Mediterranean-style Castle with its surrounding village. We parked in the lot next to an open drawbridge in a landscaped circle.

Two majestically costumed gentlemen greeted us. We were escorted to the Great Hall on the second level. A Squire took our luggage to the Guest Rooms. A brassy glass elevator that should be on a cruise ship took us there. Ahead was a man seated on a leathery swivel chair with his back to us as we entered the room, the door was sealed afterwards.

Turning, we could see the man's face - he was well-groomed, elderly, with a gray handlebar moustache that belonged in the late 1800's CE. He was dressed in the same green and yellow uniform as his Knights, with the exception of a golden crest on his lapel, in the shape of a Golden Cross.

"As you were," the man said to his escorts. The men returned to their respective stations. The man wiped his spectacles with a cloth, and then looked me over for a minute. "Hmm... So, you are the *Chosen One*, the Protector of the Shrine of AmonRa, The King of the Gods? And of course you require my assistance to defeat the enemy Apophis?"

"Yes?" I asked with indifference. The man started to laugh in a mechanical voice.

"Bravo, Sir. Bravo," he said while applauding me. "You must excuse my voice. I have this computer to focus my vocals. It's the damn Throat Cancer you see. But, you have the Amulet of AmonRa! It's the one thing that can cure me of that." He approached me from the desk in front of us.

"Sir?" I asked. He handled the Amulet and read its inscription. Then he released his grip on it.

"Yes, I was afraid of that. It seems the Amulet has taken a liking to you, Sir Michael," he replied. "Nonetheless, we will proceed."

"What would you like me to do?" I asked.

"I am the Grandmaster of the Golden Cross. My name is Sir Anu. I am to instruct you in the Ways of *Amon-Ka-Do*, the Spiritual Martial Arts of Ancient Egypt. All that I request of you is your cooperation, willpower and patience. We will be going after the most-vile of advanced society. The Army of Apophis is not some mere, *simpleton* of a terrorist organization. No, no... They are the equivalent of Carthage attacking Rome, the Hittite Empire versus Egypt, or America and the USSR. Call it what you like, it's epic," Sir Anu replied at length.

"Sir Anu, why did they go after Carmine?" I asked.

"There is something she must tell you, whenever she is ready," he said. Carmine's open mouth paused a moment while looking in my eyes.

"Michael," she started. "When we were younger, you once asked me why my eyes looked Egyptian. This was right before your interest began in Ancient Egyptian History... I have a confession to make."

"Carmine? My interest was because I felt a *strong connection* to Ancient Egypt, *not* because of *you*," I said.

"I know, I realize that... But. I am the *reincarnation* of Meryt-Aton, the daughter of the heretic-Pharaoh Akhenaton. You were never told this for *your safety*," she said in stark hesitation.

"Safety?" I asked her. "Why would I need to be *safe*?"

"You are my half-brother *Thutmosis the Fifth*. You were the heir of the King. You don't remember this because our family took you away from Egypt and gave you up. You lived in Ireland, and ruled a small Principality there. I know it sounds...crazy. I don't believe it myself. But you have to listen. I know it's hard to. There was this Prophecy that you will return to Ireland and become its High King once the Lance of AmonRa has pierced the head of Apophis," she told me nervously.

"I am a King-Arthur type? Seriously?" I asked in disbelief.

"May I?" she turned to ask Sir Anu.

"Tell him *everything*," Anu replied in his metallic voice.

"Michael, you were chosen to represent AmonRa just as Archangel Michael slays the Dragon in the Christian religion. Michael this is indeed epic, a war against Evil, and you...

You are our Hero, our *Chosen One.* You might have reservations about this subject, but you were right. Your novels are all about Ancient Egypt and AmonRa, for a good reason... Only an heir of Light can defeat the Darkness and bring back the Good in humanity. You see civilization is *crumbling* all over the World, and you think you are powerless to stop it? Well, you're *not powerless.* You have power. The Amulet *reacts* to this power. This small fact proves *who you are!"* Carmine said.

I thought a moment. "Is this why the Apophis agents are attracted to me?" I asked.

"Yes. They are *threatened* by your very presence. It's not because they are blonds or females. It's the *Yin-Yang Philosophy.* They must be opposites of Good, so the evil energies selected their positions. Michael, stay here and train with the Knights. You can trust them. The Knights told me this as I was staying in the Hospital. I was attacked because they know *who* I am now. Do this for me," she pleaded.

Chapter 8:

For the next 2 months I remained in the confines of this Castle on Cyprus, training with the *Knights of the Golden Cross*. The American Embassy renewed my passport and visa, and I had a few telephone calls to the States to make certain my plants at home were properly watered. The cabin was locked up and safe, and a friend was overseeing my emails.

I learned the **basics** of *Amon-Ka-Do*. The first level concerned itself with throws, grappling, blocks, thrusts and kicks, with emphasis on pressure points. A pressure point is like touching a nerve ending that controls a bodily function - like the base of the nose to prevent sneezing. The second level included techniques of Ancient Egyptian Stick Fighting called Tah-tib. This was accomplished with a rattan or bamboo staff, the object of which was a direct head shot, like when Set pierces the head of Apophis with a lance. Second level also includes Kendo (sword fighting), Archery (bows & arrows), and other weapons. Third level has Escape Techniques, locks (of joints), and breathing exercises with Energy Meditation. Forth level has intelligence gathering, Evasion, endurance, and various forms of boxing. The Fifth level concerns itself with thrown weapons (Shuriken, throwing knives, axes, boomerangs, etc.), telepathic Mind Control, applied psychic techniques, and conditioning. So, about 1.5 weeks per subject was my program.

On the final day I arrived in the Castle Dojo in training uniform. This was the last day and its final exam. I stood alone in the midst of a circle of some forty warriors. The bronze gong was struck three times to begin the session. They all came to me at once - a Frontal Assault. I applied the teachings of calmness in battle and resilience when confronted by numbers. Ten came to me on the left. I deflected six blows, turned, deflected seven, turned again, jumped up once and countered with a series of blocks, jabs and kicks. Another ten came to me from my right. I replicated this series, and continued with two body throws, a neck lock with my legs, and four blocks while seated. I jumped to a standing position, and then engaged in boxing while blocking non-essential blows on all angles. The last two were jump-kicks, which I avoided by quick movements. The final test was a seemingly harmless female approaching my center. I bowed, then avoided a side kick to my mask, turned around, and was attacked by a barrage of kicks. I used pressure points on her ankle to liberate her lock.

Sir Anu applauded. The warriors returned to their positions.

"Excellent, excellent! Sir Michael has improved. Now all we need is---," he stopped. A dark shadow blocked out the sunlight from the side window slits. On examination the warriors could detect a thrashing tail in the afternoon sky. It was the size of an Olympic Stadium. "Warriors! Battle Stations!"

The warriors fled to the Armory, where they removed the practice uniforms and donned Knight Armor and gambesons with yellow tunics. The shadow appeared in full view of the Sun, taunting the *Forces of Light.*

"Well Sir Michael, I surmise your formal congratulations must wait. It seems your last test is *above* us," Sir Anu replied.

I activated the *Amulet of AmonRa.* My skin darkened its usual hue, and my clothing transformed into a new form of armor, as imagined by me. I had brought along some of *my* previous Fantasy novels with me in my luggage, *for ideas.* My appearance was a gilded titanium-scaled breastplate, matching leggings, with a titanium chainmail mantle, gauntlets, and gloves. Strapped to my back were two golden-feathery wings of their own power. I held an Egyptian *Khepresh* scimitar while a Hyksos period dagger clung to my belt, along with sealed utility pouches. A communication-based helmet protected my eyes with a visor made of an unknown alloy. I could speak to our ground forces through an integrated microphone.

I stepped outside onto an adjoining balcony. Clasping my hands together as if going for a swim, I launched into the sky.

Apophis - *an agent of Apophis actually* - greeted me with a gust of cold air. This was followed by ice crystals, hail ice-balls, and dry lightning. Undeterred by his actions, I focused solar light between my fingers and stabbed him on his left wing. The light beam felt like a laser. He cried out in anguish, and then turned to my direction before spewing a large fireball at me. I crossed both of my arms into an "X", deflecting it. My eyes squinted, then I imagined the Sun becoming an eclipse. Although the Moon was nowhere close enough, I did remember that I can control the *Seasons*. The sky suddenly rained down leaves, setting his fireballs alight. The leaves scattered all over his body in the sky, clinging to him. Apophis was soon engulfed in flames. The Agent became disconnected with the amulet, and fell from her position, but parachuted down this time. The Knights captured her upon landing.

After the sky was clear, I was met by cheering knights on the ground level. The Apophis Agent was bound in special chains, and her amulet was confiscated by Sir Anu's bodyguards.

"This Agent should give us some information. Sentries, take her to the Don Jon. I will be there momentarily," Sir Anu ordered.

I lifted up the visor, and then I deactivated the *Amulet of AmonRa*, returning to normal. Sir Anu smiled and we exchanged a handshake.

"Sir Michael, I congratulate you on becoming the next *Master of Light* of the *Knighthood of the Golden Cross!* I dub thee, *Lord Michael*," Sir Anu declared. All the Knights standing behind us cheered.

I was given access to my own Tower within the Castle, as reserved for Lords and Ladies of the Order. The Tower had a private bedchamber, modern bathroom facilities, a small library or den, a medium kitchen, a practice room, storage closets, and water well.

The bedchamber came with 2-Queen size beds, some furniture, and a great view of the Knights' lands. An access trapdoor above led to the top of the Tower - in case I needed to fly away *or something.*

Chapter 9:

A knock was heard just outside the door. Carmine answered it, and then she blushed.

"Here, this is the last couple month's rent," I said to my sister as I handed her a box. She opened it. Her mouth opened up wide.

"Gold Nuggets? Where did you find them?" she asked excitedly. "Oh... not the *Amulet of AmonRa* - you used it, didn't you?"

"Yes. Call it a business expense," I said flatly. "Also here," I handed her another package, though not as nicely wrapped.

"What? A Fertility self-examination kit?" she asked. "Why?"

I projected the Amulet over her abdomen, touching her slightly. She felt something move there.

"What? *How?*" she said while walking to the bathroom. "I guess I'll have to use this... Thanks. Now I have to inform Roger that I'm artificially inseminated by an Amulet of an old Fertility God. It's not like our children are going to grow up with *Lapis Lazuli* for hair..."

"It's just adequate compensation," I replied. "For all the *good* you've done for me. All the good I am *destined* for."

"But?" she irked.

"The child *will have* Roger's DNA, okay?" I said reassuringly. "No *Lapis* hair. It's not like he's on *television* or anything."

"That reminds me," Carmine walked back into the bedroom and switched on WNN (*Washington News Network*) on the satellite television. This screen was awash with current news, most notably a large winged Dragon holding two familiar people in its talons over Seattle, WA.

"Turn this up," I ordered. The volume was increased.

"Breaking News from WNN! Someone claiming to be the Dragon Empress of a group called Apophis has taken 2 prisoners and wishes to address the public," the newswoman said.

The twisted, garbled voice was of a middle-aged female mixed with metallic background noise. Her eyes sparkled a midnight green. Her hair was a mixture of reddish brown, dirty blond and a streak of white down the middle. She had high cheekbones, fleshy lips, and an athletic physique over all. She spoke in a Western English accent, which was not heard on the television but inside Michael's mind itself.

"*AmonRa!* Return to me my children, and you can have your people back in exchange... *Or Die!"* she said. "You may find me in the *Rio de la Plaza* in Rome, Italy."

The Dragon Empress grinned, and was enveloped in a murky fog, disappearing without a trace in minutes.

"Where did she go?" Carmine demanded.

"Damn *bitch*, she teleported out!" I shouted. "She's in Italy, at the *Rio de la Plaza*."

"Who told you?" Carmine asked, perplexed.

"A voice in my mind said so," I replied while ringing my hands over my forehead in anxiety. "She got inside me and spoke to me. Some form of telepathy," I said. "Then she goes and teleports on *National Television*."

"I see," Carmine said while standing.

"Who told them where to look? The Dragon Empress doesn't know where I live!" I yelled. "What?"

Carmine knelt down at bedside, her face suddenly drawn with tears.

"Carmine? Is it something I said?" I asked quickly.

She shook her head, no. "I have a confession to make," she said.

I sat myself on the end of the bed, facing her. "Okay," I said.

"It was me. I stole the Amulet of AmonRa, AND the Amulet of Apophis. I wanted the Prophecy to come true for you, so I buried it in the ground near our home, thinking one day you would find it and become the High King of Ireland. The *Apophite* Agents followed me to Washington. That's how they found you. I - I didn't know it was you for certain," she said.

"Oh my F—ing God in Heaven! You - *you set me up!*" I said while throwing things in the emptiness of the room. Carmine dodged a thrown slipper, and then she stood up.

"It would have worked; you just needed to trust me! The Prophecy said someone with the name 'Michael' with an 'X' symbol on his body would one day claim his inheritance and become Ireland's High King. Look on your right buttocks below the waist - no, away from the mirror," she instructed. Sure enough an 'X' shaped birthmark was there.

"Well then," I said. "X *does* mark the spot."

"When you sit on the *Stone of Destiny* the birthmark lights up," she informed me. "The *Stone of Destiny* is what drew me to you as a child. My memories of Meryt-Aton with the Prophecy inspired me to keep this a family secret until the right time. And *now* you know."

"So where is the *Rio de la Plaza?*" I asked her.

"It's a nightclub near the Arena. Top floor," she smiled. "Good luck."

Chapter 10:

Old Mediterranean-styled buildings with red tile rooftops, solid walls of plastered-over-stucco, and Italian artwork stood on a sloping hillside. Nearby was this ancient Arena where lions and gladiators once fought for the pleasure of Roman Magistrates or an adoring, bloodthirsty Republic. I *teleported* into a Roman Bathhouse, currently closed due to renovation.

I walked outside to inhale the clean air of modern Rome. A number of blond Apophite Agents started motorcycle engines upon my appearance. They had been waiting for me.

I ran to the nearest tourist rental, and popped the dealer a gold nugget the size of a standard Golf ball. He smiled in confusion as I selected a *Vespa* Motor-scooter with helmet and drove off amid the traffic behind me. *Driving here wasn't as easy as a popular fictional British spy would have one believe.* There were short connected roads intersecting other lanes, with no serious civil planning established. So I switched to the Public thoroughfares, the ones with traffic lights and road signs.

I placed a flagpole in between two fish market trays set against an entrance to a short tunnel, so that the pursuing Agents behind me would collide into it. I also made a simple smoke-screen fashioned from burning pitch coupled with lavish incense. This worked while driving into and through an open Church. Three Apophite Agents dismounted and climbed this pole leading to a tall water tower, waiting for me to pass by in an effort to land on my guest seat. One succeeded, and she tried to knock me off the *Vespa* by clawing my eyes from behind me. So I deliberated crashed the *Vespa* into a truck hauling fertilizer, sideways down. Then I got back up, and drove until I reached this cliff. I escalated the *Vespa*, grabbed my Amulet of AmonRa, and drove off with 4 Motorcycles in pursuit, also over the cliff where they exploded on the rocks below. The Amulet teleported me directly into the desired Nightclub once I found its address by driving around and noticing the City signs.

"Ah, the *Rio de la Plaza* Nightclub," I exhaled. "It's also called the *Dark Harem*." I walked around until I found a servant's uniform on a wheeled tray, so I wore it as a disguise. I didn't see any hidden cameras. But that's probably why they're hidden.

Women in various guises existed here, as no men were allowed in. I noticed women had their own exercise and sparring rooms, wrestling matches, and boxing tournaments. The lap pool was also private, with a steam room, Jacuzzi, and heated pool. Most of these women had artificially blond hair, though I did notice hair colorants in the restroom. A secret room I accidentally found by leaning up against a panel in one wall. The windows had one-way glass, so a mirror appeared on the opposite side. In here were computers, and a Genetic Modification room - rows of females with wires and tubes inserted into them, slept in capsules. Colorful liquids bubbled in canisters amid dark green goop and sticky confections with the scent of Lavender and Lotus blossoms.

I found one computer printout left on the floor. In reading it (in Italian) I noticed numerous references to Alexandria, Egypt. They have a base there, it seems. The printout even supplied an accurate address. I crumpled it up and stored it.

While walking along the hidden room my right foot hit a trap button on the tile floor, which opened up. I slid down this hidden slide for about 5 seconds until reaching a room. The bottom led to a room filled with Styrofoam pellets. I pulled myself off the slide.

In landing I collided into a woman with alternate hair features and athletic legs. "Oops," I remarked.

The Dragon Empress spoke, "And here I wish I had snakes for hair." The Amulet of Apophis that rested on *her* breast was unlike the other ones; this one was thought-controlled. Her hair transformed into garter snakes.

I crawled to a stand.

"No, you *must be* seated," she said after knocking me down via a kick to the face. "There. *Now* you return to me my Agent or those two will have a new fate of their own..." She pointed to two people on her left. They had been hanging onto a rope over a pool filled with electric eels originally from Egypt. It was Roger and Si-Hithor. Both had gauze on their mouth, and their wrists were tied to the rope. I waved slightly. Roger motioned a smile. Si-Hithor frowned in disapproval.

"Ah, the Amulet of AmonRa. I've always wanted it," the Dragon Empress said as she snatched it off my neck. But then she noticed something else.

"What? WHAT?" she demanded.

My skin was still bronzed and my clothes were still armor. Nothing changed despite her having the Amulet.

"You forgot about deception, Your Majesty," I said from behind her. I turned off the Fake Me using the *real* Amulet of AmonRa. I switched while sliding down into the room. Then I activated the Multiplicity Feature, which caused my image to multiply into many separate forms. With each form she attacked, another took its place. She was too busy attacking these deceptions to notice I had cut down Roger and Si-Hithor and escaped via a hidden stairwell.

"How *long* were you *up* there?" I asked Roger and Si-Hithor.

"For the past hour, those electric eels looked *tasty*," Roger said.

"I forgot - he's a *Chef*," I related to Si-Hithor. She grinned slightly.

"So, what's the *Game Plan*? Do we have *one*?" Si-Hithor asked.

I exchanged glances with Roger. "Not really. Roger knows Aikido and you are familiar with mixed-Martial Arts... Why not just *fight* our way out?" I said.

"There are *hundreds* of them!" Roger complained.

"Sounds good to me," Si-Hithor smiled while cracking her knuckles.

On the way to the Pool area, we raided a storage locker full with silent weapons - mostly throwing stars, blades, axes and a few staves. The locker also had 3 Kevlar vests with titanium plates added. So we armed ourselves appropriately. Si-Hithor preferred the staves and the throwing axes. Roger took up the throwing stars and Sai daggers. I activated my Amulet of AmonRa for effect.

A blond Apophite Agent met us at the Pool room entrance, wearing swimming pants and a Serpent necklace. She saw me coming and slammed her fist onto a red Emergency button, setting off the alarm. Si-Hithor silenced her with a thrown Axe to her cranium.

"Good shot," I replied. "Ready?"

"Ready," Roger and Si-Hithor said in unison.

The Swimming Pool area was on alert. Blond Agents scrambled about, pushing floor panels around to reveal hidden stashes of weapons and armor. The Pool itself had an automatic clear lid sealing it shut. The Agents attempted to attack us as we marched down the aisle, throwing bladed weapons and repelling blows with our walking sticks. An Agent appeared in front of me, so Si-Hithor kicked her down, locking her neck in a *Jujitsu* embrace using her legs. As the Agent was knocked unconscious I noticed something curious about a tag appearing just along her neck.

"What is this tag for? *Made in China?"* I asked Si-Hithor. So I pulled it off. This opened a *panel* inside her neck, full of computer parts and Silicon chips. The hidden room now made sense to me, the one with the blond agents sleeping inside capsules.

"Oh my F—ing god, *they're all machines!"* I exclaimed. "All of them!"

"Clones?" Roger asked.

"More likely ***Shabtis,***" Si-Hithor realized. "They're not alive, just **animated statues**... *Like the ones in Ancient Egyptian tombs!"*

The Blond Agents heard that. I threw down the mechanical corpse and imagined larger weapons, which appeared momentarily later.

"You have a machine gun?" Si-Hithor asked, startled.

"Here are yours," I said while handing them each one. Then I loaded the ammunition and pointed towards the crowd of angry blond automatons in front of us.

"It's party time at poolside!" I ordered. We took our time flooring these automatons, in back and forth movements of the assault rifles. Bullets ripped through the robotic Shabtis, and shattered the back glass walls. Some even fell into the sealed swimming pool or Jacuzzi. This lasted about 20 minutes.

The rising dust, computer steam, and stench of burnt wires were the only items left moving here. We found the exit door. It had a computer security lock on it, so I shot it several times with the machine gun until it opened. The exit was five meters away. It was blocked by emergency doors that descended from the alarm.

"That's okay. I didn't arrive in Italy that way," I said. I held the Amulet of AmonRa to form a *False Door* along one blank wall for teleportation back to the Shrine of AmonRa in Alexandria, Egypt. We entered it after securing the room from any blond automatons following us. The *False Door* disappeared moments after we entered the Shrine.

Chapter 11:

A week later, I was asleep in the Tower on Cyprus. The time was after 2:00 am, and I had difficulty sleeping, because of a **dream**. Images filtered through my mind - stark images, of buildings, of royalty and of this one *woman*. She appeared in my room as I dreamt her into existence, like a *succubus*. Her muscular bronzed legs lay astride my abdomen, as her hands massaged my chest, arms, and head - forcing my head into her bosom, repeatedly. Her lips rubbed against my neck erotically, and then her tongue licked my neck, face, and other *lower regions*. She held me down as if trying to *force an erection*, but by this time I *awoke* - she was as a Spirit fastening me to the bedposts with her hands. I couldn't move. Then I noticed a medium Serpent tattoo on her neck. I summoned the Amulet of AmonRa on my nightstand. She looked at it: her eyes suddenly alight with orange fire, and her mouth angrily motioning towards me. The hair on her head changed into slithering black Asps. I stared into those fiery orange eyes, the heat of her bodily form dripping with perspiration. Her hands continued to rub and sensually grasp my sex organ until an *orgasm* occurred; and then she leaned backwards and laughed. But this time her body transformed into a Black Dragon and disappeared in a burst of white fog. The *dream* soon expired.

I awoke an hour later. It was about 3:30am. The night sky outside the Tower was overcast with some stars visible. A comet or meteor lit up the sky with its orange tail streaking in the horizon. Inside the Tower I walked down its spiral staircase to the Library, using a flashlight. The shelves had these dusty glass cases protecting some aged tomes from a variety of archaic subjects. One concerned itself with Medieval Cooking, another about Dragons and Knights; one was about the Holy Grail. The one most interesting to me discussed the Prophecy of the *Stone of Destiny*. So I switched on an electric lamp and read the book until early dawn.

I walked down to the main kitchen in the Castle. Sir Anu, Sir Lucas, Roger, and Carmine dined in the Great Hall for breakfast. The aged wooden table served up to 20 Knights at one time. Sir Anu was seated in the middle with Sir Lucas on his right. Two servants supplied food, drink, and utensils. The food was given in pure silver vessels, polished enough to see one's reflection in them. Fresh chicken, bagels, Eggs Benedict, toast, orange and cranberry juices, porridge, and a side order of Falafel were served.

The Knights ate breakfast in their uniforms, and returned to their civil duties as was their routine. I was seated near Carmine to her right. She commented on my choice of clothing – I was dressed in a Blacksmith's tunic, with dark pants and shoes. It was the only attire in the closet that was *black*. And I *like* black. She was arrayed in fine Phoenician purple. Roger wore a Nobleman's doublet found in the Castle Armory, made of green corduroy and gilded brass buttons. Carmine would *prefer* I wear more *royal* clothing, befitting my future status as *High King*.

"So what is so wrong about exploring *your birthright?*" Carmine asked between bites. "It's better than being a *starving writer* of fantasy fiction."

"I like writing, *not* living what I write," I replied. Carmine gave me that *stare*, as if I don't know anything. "What?"

"Sir Lucas, do you happen to serve Milk?" Carmine asked politely.

"Yes milady, we serve Cow's Milk and various Cheeses, as well," Sir Lucas replied happily. He snapped his fingers to the servants in response.

"I like Milk *on my porridge*, Michael," Carmine said while cutting a slice of *Sharp Cheddar*.

"I thought *Commoners* drank Milk, Lady Carmine," I mocked.

Her fork hit the dish rather loudly. Then she cleared her throat.

"Well, Lord Michael, Bulls were once the *patron* of Pharaohs. Like the Mighty Bull *Nebkheperura*," she added. "Or perhaps the Apis Bulls of Lord Ptah were once worshiped as Gods?"

"Who cleaned the stables but *women* maidservants?" I suggested.

"You would be so lucky, *Prince Thutmosis*, who never once ruled Egypt," Carmine said while eating a bagel. "I'm surprised the memory lapse has not reached your temporal lobe yet."

"Pharaonic Monuments made of stone *may last* for thousands of years, but a book in the mouth of its reader *lasts forever*," I said. "The quote is from the *18th Dynasty*, Lady Carmine. *Your Dynasty*, I believe."

"*Our* Dynasty, Lord Michael. *Don't forget* that part," she smiled.

"*Fruit* would be nice," I suggested.

"Lord Michael, if I may... Why did you seek the kitchen so early in the morning?" Sir Anu asked.

"I couldn't sleep," I said.

"Was the bed not comfortable? I can alleviate that," Sir Anu asked.

"No, the bed is very nice. I had this dream about a woman who was having intercourse with me, and then she turned into a Black Dragon," I said.

"In *our* Castle! How *dare* she?" Sir Anu exploded. "Do you know? No, of course not, you're too young and inexperienced," he said.

"Truly," Sir Lucas explained. "This is an attack on our fortifications and cannot be let alone."

"Servants, *bring in* some Coffee," Sir Anu replied at length. "Lord Michael, please excuse my outburst a moment ago... The Legend of the Black Dragon is as ancient as the *Stone of Destiny*. This cannot be ignored as trivial. The Black Dragon takes the *semen* from a Prince of Light and fashions an Archenemy with it. The legend inspired an Arthurian story in later generations about a bastard son of the King who gave Arthur a mortal wound in combat. Now this Dragon came to *you* after you defeated her Empress. The Empress is *not* the leader of the Apophite Army. Those Shabtis do the bidding of the Black Dragon *herself*."

"Then the Black Dragon *is* Apophis?" I asked Sir Anu.

"No. Apophis is a Spirit and is immortal, meaning he never dies. The Black Dragon is also immortal, but *she has a weakness* that can render her powerless when properly hit. The bone connecting the spine to the neck must be severed with a lance, preventing reattachment. It's her Achilles' Heel - there is a *book* in your Tower library that talks about this," Sir Anu explained.

"I think there is a picture of this in many Egyptology bookstores. The image of Set spearing Apophis the Dragon comes to mind," I said. "Set touches the head of the Dragon with the spear, preventing it from attacking. The same applies to Archangel Michael or St. George."

"Yes. This is real, you do *know* that?" Sir Anu paused.

"Of course I do. I am also taking notes. This would make one heck of a novel," I replied.

"Carmine, it's time. Meet us in the Armory," Sir Anu said while finishing the meal.

"What?" I asked as everyone was leaving the room.

"We have to *show* you something," Sir Anu said excitedly.

Chapter 12:

The midday Sun poured into the Castle via arrow slits in the shape of Crosses. Within the Armory were 15 fully dressed Knights, Sir Lucas, Sir Anu, Carmine, Roger, and myself - all awaiting this 'surprise.'

"Do you wish to do the honors, Sir Lucas?" Sir Anu asked.

"Certainly Sir Anu," Sir Lucas replied as he cut a ribbon securing this heavy, cast iron door plated in bronze with the insignia of a Dragon being pierced by a lance-wielding *Knight of the Golden Cross*.

The door flipped open revealing a long dusty object, wrapped in ancient linen. Sir Lucas picked it up and removed its sheath. Inside was a metallic weapon of Ancient Egyptian origin, resembling a two-headed spear.

"The Lance of AmonRa!" Sir Anu responded. "And this now belongs to you, *Lord Michael*," Sir Anu said as he offered the lance to me.

The Lance was fashioned of *Orichalcum* with gemstones and golden hieroglyphs. Its twin blades are of the same metal alloy, a prized metal from *Ancient Atlantis - the Domain of the Gods*. It was 100 times stronger than Steel, and ¼ its weight comparably.

The sunlight bounced off each blade like water from a waterfall. I accepted the gift with much appreciation. Now, it is time to test it.

Satellite television from Alexandria, Egypt, showed a series of Apophite Agents working in the sky over Abydos. Twelve Dragons were spotted there, with one bearing the insignia of the *Servitude of the Dragon Empress* in turquoise.

"Lord Michael, the *Empress* has been sighted at Abydos, Egypt. An opportunity presents itself," Sir Lucas told me from the Communications Room in the Castle.

"I will set up a *False Door* here and then teleport over. You can follow me when ready," I replied. "The *Empress* is mine." I placed the Lance on a shoulder strap on my back, and then entered the teleport to Abydos within minutes.

Abydos, the City of Lord Osiris, the God of the Afterlife for much of Ancient Egypt and Rome - this city is sacred. Now it is *desecrated* by the presence of Apophite Agents. But that may *change*.

The Dragons all saw me enter the City, so they made a circle around the Osirion as their tournament. Their challenger was the *Empress* herself, who stood her ground wearing a simple two-piece outfit resembling a swim suit. She took off the Amulet of Apophis, to fight me without cheating. This prompted me to do the same. I placed the Amulet of AmonRa on a stone ledge for safety.

"A wise decision, *Lord Michael*," the Empress said in a reptilian accent with a hint of Latin. Reptilian accents tend to sound like a loaded tongue not a hiss. "I will be *easy* on you, flesh-ling."

She started with a vertical kick to my head, knocking me off balance. She was only 5 foot eleven to my 6 foot four inches in height. Then she thrust a palm strike to my face, turned and did a spiral kick back up and across my jaw. My lower lip bled somewhat as I wiped it with my fist.

She smiled on seeing blood. "Aha, you are *not* immortal, eh Lord Michael?"

I punched her in a forward strike to her smiling face, knocking her off balance. Then I blocked two lateral kicks, repelled a jab to my kidneys and blocked a throat strike. I closed in on her, and pushed two pressure points on her face, causing her to back off. She slapped me with her right palm, and then spiral kicked my face to the ground where she jumped on my left shoulder. A short kick across my jaw by her foot caused me to move sideways, preventing her from trampling me again. I stood up only to be flipped over her left shoulder, and caught in a leg lock. I clawed her leg with my right hand. I heard her doing something else, but I couldn't see anything. Then I felt something injected into my neck.

"What is that?" I gasped.

"Oh this? It's Genetic Poison made from your semen. It's a gift from the Black Dragon. It only affects you," She said in defiance.

"What...does...it...do?" I coughed.

"Oh nightmares, chills, hallucinations, pain, and a fever," she said.

After the poison was injected she released me from the Jujitsu leg lock and let me stand up. Then she jump-kicked me in the face, knocking me unconscious; I awoke on the desert floor in Abydos.

I tried standing up. My vision was blurred and I was dizzy. I searched for the *Amulet of AmonRa*, but I couldn't find it. That was my *only* ticket home. I did see the Lance - it was stuck on a rock in the distance. There was about 100 meters between the Lance and myself. I had to get my bearings first.

A Dust Storm appeared and surrounded me. Limping, I managed to crawl to the Osirion with the assistance of a small stick I found. Minutes seemed like hours.

There I was at the Osirion. The Lance was within my grasp. Then something hit me from behind, hard.

"Do you really think I am done with you?" the Empress said sarcastically. She turned me around and kneed me in the stomach, then kneed my head upwards, and trampled my face onto the brickwork of the Osirion before pushing my motionless body into the pool below. I sank about 3 feet underwater. I saw her smile and turned to walk away in absent victory.

The water was cool and inviting. I lay on the bottom of the pool, holding my breath. Then as I thought everything was over, I felt a hand reach in and pull me out. It was Carmine.

She started yelling at me about leaving me alone with those monsters. Then she started to lecture about how Ancient Egypt was detrimental to my health. I offered to say something.

"Yes? What is it?" Carmine demanded.

"The *Osirion* has healing powers," I said meekly. "I'm cured."

"Well that's good. It's not like you--," she stopped. "What do you *mean* you're cured?"

I swallowed some of it actually. It's like the water from the Styx River in Ancient Greek Mythology, or from the Christian Holy Grail. I was cured from Mortality. It's like a *Panacea Vaccine.*

"Plus I have something of hers," I said while pulling out a business card that fell during the battle. It had an address over in Ireland. This was the location of the *Black Dragon* herself.

We recovered the Lance but not the Amulet of AmonRa. We believe the Empress has it or took it to her boss. So we boarded the next flight out to Ireland. We arrived within 1 week's time.

Chapter 13:

I made some modifications to the *Lance of AmonRa*. I allowed the spearheads to retract for easier movement. Sir Anu accompanied us to Ireland via Cyprus. I needed his advice.

Tracking the *Black Dragon* down wasn't that difficult as Dragons were seen in her region. That the Apophite-Dragon Agents were all Shabtis didn't alarm me. The *Empress* worried me - was she human or an immortal? Or was she also a *Shabty* programmed by the *Black Dragon* or even Apophis himself?

It wasn't just them that worried me. News stories all over the Earth had problems. There were daily school shootings, daily bombings or terrorist attacks against other Governments. People stopped going to Churches, the youthful embraced Atheism and Islam, or Science. Anarchist groups influenced Cities, and crime rates soared. All of these events happened because of the negative influence or hostile energies coming from Apophis and its Agents on Earth. If he were to be defeated or vanquished, would all this activity stop?

We arrived at a small Castle owned by a cousin of Sir Anu whom was away for the seasons. The Castle had a guest room for our use. Sir Anu decided to accommodate himself in the Castle's bedchamber, as it was fortified.

A local elderly woman saw Carmine and approached her.

"Pardon Milady, but... do you know the descendants of Scota?"

"Uhm... Scota?" asked Carmine. "No, but I was Princess Meryt-aton in a previous life."

The woman looked shocked. "May I?" she asked. "The person whom you identify with *is Scota*, the Founder of Ireland, according to Legend. Tell me, *what do you think of that?"*

"Uh...we are here to combat a Dragon Queen *with our sorcery*. Does anyone in the village know about the *Black Dragon*?" I asked her.

The woman's eyes bulged, and then she bowed all the way to the ground. "I am not worthy, *your Majesty*."

"Michael, *leave her alone*," Carmine snapped.

"Michael is it? The Prophecy! *The Prophecy!"* said the woman as she fled the vicinity.

"Lord Michael," Sir Anu interrupted. "The locals have a better *understanding* of the situation than we realize. I suggest not catering to their ideology too deeply."

"*Over-stood*, Sir," I nodded.

We took a car ride across the region to a pastureland site. We avoided people on the right side of the road, knowing it was the reverse side of traffic as in the States. We reached the township of *Blarney* by evening. I had a feeling of anticipation about this site, and while the others were fixing the car (it had rained and we had the windows down) **I sat down on a slab of protruding sandstone mixed with basalt**. My ass started to tingle, and I felt unusually hot. So I stood up and walked back to the car.

We then drove back to the Castle. Carmine noticed something on my pants.

"Michael, I was wondering something," she said. "Why is your *birthmark* glowing?"

I looked at it from another mirror. "Well I don't really know. What could this be?" I said.

Carmine studied my eyes carefully. I wasn't dishonest. "Well, the Prophecy said, '*Unless the fates be faulty grown, and prophet's voice be vain, wherever is found this sacred stone, the Scottish race shall reign.*' Did you happen to **sit on any stones** while we were traveling?"

"Yes. Here, I photographed it on my Tablet Computer," I remarked.

Carmine's eyes widened. "Where was this stone?"

"At Blarney, I think. Why?" I asked her.

"Hmm... *Blarney*," she mumbled. "No reason," she smiled.

Chapter 14:

Three days later, we approached the large Castle occupied by the Dragons. You could see Dragon Agents guarding the Towers, hovering above in the sky. Each Dragon had this mysterious fog aura around them. The locals said a secret entrance tunnel ran under the Main Gates and its surrounding Walls. So we entered a tunnel that had this bronze grating over it. Sir Anu brought a blow-torch with its gas-powered generator. This took time to cut into, at about 20 minutes.

The tunnel was murky, slippery with eons of sludge. There were rats of course. This passage led to an ancient sewage center in the heart of the Castle, but above panels allowed a passageway that had eye slits for viewing. Each eye slit was behind the eyes in painted murals in one of the rooms. Carmine whispered to me about what I witnessed.

"I see two Dragons, and...wait, I see the *Empress*. She's talking to a few blond *Shabtis*," I **whispered**. "The *Shabtis* are holding an object."

"Will you be *needing* this?" Sir Anu asked me while holding the *Lance*.

"Yes, in a bit," I said **aloud**. "We still need to..."

An explosion threw me from the observatory ledge where the paintings were. I landed on a pile of sludge. Apparently the Empress has excellent hearing. Two Dragons accompanied her into the secret passage.

"Well, well. We have in our midst the *High King of Ireland*. Your Majesty, Lord Michael, *prepare to die*," the Empress said in haste.

"Wait - *what* did you just call me?" I implored.

"Your *birthmark* signaled everyone of your new status when you sat on the *Stone of Destiny* a few days ago. *Everyone knows*," the Empress said.

I turned to Carmine. She smiled back and nodded affirmatively.

"Then I order you to *submit*. You may *kiss the floor* if you wish," I ordered. Then I leaned back and threw the Lance at her. The Lance penetrated the base of her neck, causing her to fall backwards into the wall crater. "When I said '*kiss the floor*' it wasn't an option."

The other two Dragons attacked Carmine and Sir Anu. I ran towards the Empress, who was holding the end of the Lance with its spearhead still inside her neck. Her fiery eyes looked at me with anger. I pulled on the Lance, but it didn't budge so I twisted it around until her head fell off, and rolled down the steps. Inside her neck were computer wires, microchips and flashing lights - no blood or human veins. The *Empress* was an automaton after all.

"No hard feelings, then. Carmine, throw the water from Abydos into their eyes," I said. "It will *deactivate* them."

Carmine deflected a few blows, two kicks, and a jab to her throat from a Dragon. She reached into her belt pouch and retrieved a vial of Osirion Water from the pool in Abydos. As the Dragon clutched Carmine's neck with one hand, smiling evilly, Carmine gouged its eye and then poured the water into it. Then she backed off to watch.

The Dragon appeared as if poisoned. The blond hair on its head transformed into white, its skin from youthfulness into elderly wrinkles. The Dragon's face became a white-washed skull and when the body fell onto the stonework floor, it shattered like pottery.

"Next?" Carmine asked the other Dragon, who upon seeing this, fled the room in a foggy departure.

I retrieved the detached head of the *Empress*, and we followed the other Dragon all the way to the Great Hall of the Castle. Carmine found the *Amulet of AmonRa* from the fallen Dragon, and gave it to me.

The Great Hall was a throne room, dining hall, and a bedroom. In this case, the *Black Dragon* ordered her Government of *Shabtis*. She was waiting for me. Four Dragons guarded the entrance and after I entered they sealed the doors, trapping me inside. Carmine and Sir Anu watched helplessly from the windows.

"So, the *High King* wants a parley with the Black Dragon?" she asked.

"No, just your head to add to my collection," I told her as I withdrew the head of the *Empress* before tossing it at her feet. Her face became pale at this sight. Then her mouth cringed in hatred.

I activated the Amulet of AmonRa and prepared the Lance. The Black Dragon removed her black cloak, revealing her athletic bodily form. She was dressed in translucent black silk, with black Italian high-heels. Her hair was composed of slithering black Asps, as revealed when she removed this serpent crown from her head.

"So, I am Yin and you are Yang. Our fated fight-to-the-death was heralded long *before* your birth, *High King*," the Black Dragon said as we prepared to fight.

"We are similar," I said.

"We are NOT alike! You are a Mortal, and I am Immortal and shall reign forever..." The Black Dragon said.

"Do you remember the *Osirion*?" I asked while opening a vial of water.

"Of course I remember it! I am the Black Dragon, consort of Apophis, the Egyptian God of Darkness!" She shouted in anger. She approached me.

"The Waters heal and grant Immortality. Here, *try some*," I said as I splashed the water into her eyes, causing them to sting. She grabbed her eyes with both hands, screaming until all the windows along the walls cracked.

I leaned back and threw the Lance into her neck, but she caught it with one hand. In her now blurred vision she saw me advance. So she kicked every image of me that was visible, missing me entirely.

"You're getting old, *Lady of Darkness*. You can't fight me forever," I taunted. "Submit now and I will consider your surrender."

"Never!" She announced. She approached me with the Lance embedded in her right shoulder. Both hands were free to attack me.

I struck first, hitting her larynx. Then I pummeled her with blows to her face, shoulder, spleen and abdomen. She deflected all blows except to the face, where I managed to bruise both her eyes. Her mouth opened up and launched a fireball to me. I crossed my arms and deflected it. She kicked my head twice, and I fell briefly onto the blood-soaked floor. As she raised her left foot over my head as if to crush it, I grabbed a hold of the Lance. She started to trample my head with that foot as I felt along the shaft of the Lance for the special button I added recently.

Her face was now visible behind her arched foot, and she seemed almost happy.

"Good bye, Lord Michael!" she said upon delivering a final blow.

I pressed the button that released the other spearhead into her neck. She forced her weight on my head using her foot, and in doing so caused the spearhead to penetrate her neck where the spine connects. Then she felt great pain and fell aside me. I was safe.

I crawled to a standing position. The Black Dragon became motionless. I poured the remnant of the Osirion Water onto her face, which caused steam to emanate.

Outside the Castle, the formerly overcast and cloudy sky dissipated into clear and sunny weather. People from all over the World changed. School shootings and police assaults stopped. Terrorism ended when all the terrorists suddenly died of heart attacks or strokes. Churches regained followers, and the young no longer sought corrupt behavior. Companies realized profit didn't matter over quality of work, and helping people became more a priority. The Countries of Earth all sought coexistence, peace and Justice. The *Curse of Apophis* has ceased.

The Castle doors opened up as the *Shabtis* Army deactivated. Carmine ran towards me, crying and laughing at the same time. Sir Anu waved his right hand as a salute, wearing his Knightly Armor and uniform.

Chapter 15: Epilogue

The weather was sunny on the beach along a Red Sea resort. Someone built sand castles and sand pyramids, strengthened with sea water. A young child played with inflatable toys without fear of the tides, now that sharks kept their distance.

Back in Ireland I was invested with royal power as the new *High King of Ireland* - an office I *shared* with the older royals in England proper. The Prophecy had been fulfilled. For their acts of assistance and courage, I incorporated the *Knights of the Golden Cross* into my new Government. Sir Anu was also compensated with a museum piece - a Tablet Computer image of the pierced Black Dragon. ***I also cured his Throat Cancer***. The Black Dragon herself was moved to a Castle tower with the Lance of AmonRa permanently embedded in her neck, to prevent evil from affecting the Living. There she will remain, with sunlight entering through the tower windows every morning, striking her wound with its energy and empowering *Goodness* everywhere.

Carmine lived in my Cabin in Washington. The rent was paid up. A copy of my newest book rested comfortably on a pedestal in the Living Room. Its title was, "*AmonRa: God of Kings, King of Gods*." And it was a best-seller for many years to come...

About the Author:

Horus Michael follows the training of Ancient Egyptian Priests in his varied works on the Occult. He also studies Egyptian Archaeology. He currently lives in California, USA.

www.amazon.com/author/horusmichael

www.amazon.com/author/michaeljcosta

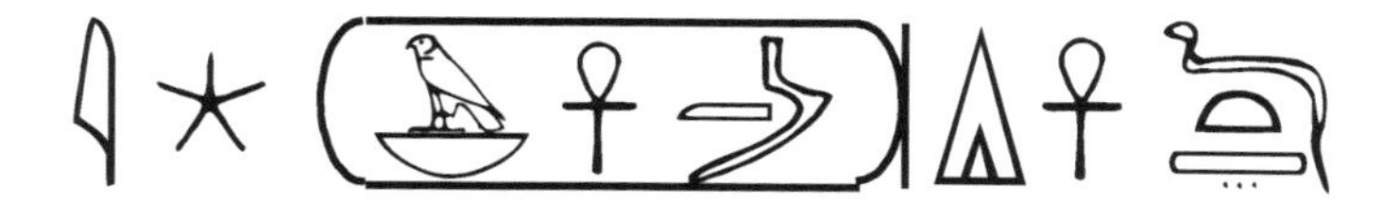

Bast the Cat Goddess

And the Tomb of the Emerald Pharaoh

Bast the Cat Goddess

And the Tomb of the Emerald Pharaoh

Michael J. Costa

Bast the Cat Goddess

And the Tomb of the Emerald Pharaoh

This book was printed in the U.S.A.

(6"x9" B&W)

Acknowledgement:

The Author would like to thank the publishers and editors of this and all future editions of this work. Also thanks to http://www.per-bast.org/ for research, to the *Goddess Bast* for inspiration, and to my family for their support.

For: John E. Morby and his Cat, Sety.

And for Bast herself.

January 19, 2011

On board the *Athena* as it cruised the Nile River in Egypt:

I was never a man for gossip, being a billionaire playboy who fancies himself quite the Archaeologist. Okay, so it was an honorary doctorate from donating to the Golden Cross, but still... The locals here claim there was a rebellion over in nearby Tunisia - again this *must* be gossip. I was safe here in Lower Egypt. My yacht, the *Athena*, just had its deck cleaned and the maintenance bill was not scheduled for another week - perfect time to catch up with a round of golf on the forward deck.

A servant entered from the promenade deck carrying his usual offering of neatly pressed khakis, white leathery loafers, and a glass of mint ice tea with the standard paper umbrella found in local restaurants. I had just left the Jacuzzi for a dip in the cool, 7-foot deep tomb of a swimming pool. It was the one with a large effigy of Ramses the Great lacquered as a pool mural. The servant placed his offering on a slim resin table, aside my Acer laptop with external solar battery. I was keeping up to date with my Company stock portfolios.

"Doctor Costa? Madame wishes to know when you will be ready for the excursion you planned this evening. Madame wants to know if you will need another case of golf balls. It seems the last case is being used for floats by the local fisherman," the servant said.

"Ah yes, of course. You may tell Madame Julia I will be ready in an hour," I told him. He smiled slightly. My publicist, Ms. Julia Silversmith, wants to tour the lower ruins of Bubastis soon for research and to entertain some guests.

A few minutes passed while I changed into *less* comfortable attire. I reached down to the plastic Tee, placed a small white ball onto its base, reached back and swung my 8-iron. The ball entered the Nile along one embankment.

"Ah yes, another fisherman float; what *will* they think of next?" I remarked.

An hour and one half an hour later, I appeared below deck ready for anything. My trademark utility jacket, crisp baseball cap (*Go Giants!*), and laser pointer in hand went well with the group I was to lead on this auspicious tour of the Cat cemetery of *Tell Basta*.

Madame Julia, escorted by her entourage of funky techno-scribes, followed my lead. The crypts were especially damp this evening. Last night's winter mist may be to blame. The group was informed not to overly incorporate flash bulb photography in the ruins, as excessive light will cause painted murals to fade. Though most images were of myself, as some members sought my autograph.

My unusually large flashlight, not yet strobe material, flickered against the walls like a story from a campfire ritual. No horror stories here, I thought. Unless you were of course a cat - and was sacrificed to *Bast the Cat Goddess*. This was seen as a pious offering to some now decadent ancient religion. It was also how domestic cats came into existence. My group heard that part last.

I entered a recently excavated room, and then without warning the floor gave way. This was not uncommon for this to occur here in Egypt, for many discoveries are accidental. My fall of four meters was cushioned by the bandaged mummies stacked against the stone floor, amid a fountain of inhalable dust, to which I sneezed three times.

Julia asked me if I was all right before noticing a strange light coming from the room before me. She pointed in the aforementioned direction. My eyes followed her gaze, and then I found a likeness of some hideous beast in the form of a gazing, open-mouthed mummified corpse, which caused me to scream.

Recovering, I climbed to my stance and proceeded into the next room, expecting enlightenment. The light in question emanated from a small box of gilded Cedar-wood in the shape of an Ankh Mirror case. I once found a photograph of the one owned by the *Golden Pharaoh*, but this one was more artistically carved. The box creaked open as my eager fingers dug into its curved shape and dusty handle. It contained one small, linen-wrapped object. I picked it up while trying to read the faint inscription coarsely written on the wrappings.

"Doctor Costa! Do you need help?" asked Julia.

"I found something! I will be a minute..." I replied.

My left hand slipped into my utility jacket's front pocket to retrieve my sturdy cell phone, for a digital photograph. "Good, three sections in Bitmaps. I will have to decipher this later."

"What is this?"I asked a bulging shape in the mess of aged linen.

The shape, it turns out, was a small stone **amulet** in the shape and contours of a sacred Cat. Approximately four inches of a black stone, almost obsidian or possibly onyx, the **amulet** was chosen for its slick representation of Cat fur. The dark luster reflected in my electric torch light. Above the image were two, very small *emeralds* for eyes. The **amulet** hook above was connected to a cord that kept its security intact, and was still wearable.

On the reverse side of the **amulet** was an inscription, possibly *Third Intermediate Period* glyphs. There was a cartouche in which the name of "*Bast-en-ka-nefer*" figured prominently. I immediately called out to Julia to cast down a rope ladder to retrieve me. I noticed one on the way over here.

The rope ladder was sturdy enough to support my weight. Julia greeted me with some hesitation. A gentleman in a dark pinstripe overcoat with the badge of an official of some sort emblazoned on this also greeted me with some hesitation.

"Dr. Costa?" asked the gentleman.

"Yes?" I replied. "Have I broken the law or just the floor here?"

"Dr. Costa, I am a representative of the **Supreme Council of Antiquities** in Egypt. Your work on the translation of the *Taharqa Stone* has set an example of new technologies that we of Egypt aspire to. I would like to invite you to visit a new site in Saqqara that may be of some interest to you and your company."

"So the floor is not a problem?" I stonewalled the official.

"No. Not at all, Doctor," smiled Ahmed the Head of the SCA of Saqqara, or so read his badge on his suit's left flank. "We knew the floor was unstable already. Didn't you see the warning plaques?"

I placed the amulet of Bast around my neck, hidden below my jacket. I would have to decipher it another time. The official led me away from the group, but then they seemed more interested in the free ice cream being presented by the SCA catering truck that just arrived. Julia smiled over three scoops of Vanilla and Caramel topping. The evening sun still clocked over 80F in the shade.

Ahmed handed me a print-out of a diagram and a tablet computer display for my perusal. In the 3D blueprints on the tablet I noticed a subterranean structure, shaped like a 3rd Dynasty coffin - the archaic "palace style." There was no opening on the exterior, nor on the printed out satellite map. I asked him about this.

"No, there is no apparent entryway into the structure," Ahmed explained.

"What of a hidden niche or blocked passageways?" I asked.

"We thought of that, actually. There are three," he pointed, "Here, here and there. The triangles are probably plastered over niches. As they are inaccessible due to the limestone covering, we will have to excavate it."

I looked over the tablet and into Ahmed's eyes. He seemed a bit fearful for a second, as if indecision loomed. "Ahmed, what are we looking for in here?" I asked. "Is it a tomb?"

"That's why I brought you, the linguist. Your company translated the *Taharqa Stone* using algorithms whose properties no one has since rivaled. I insist you come and explore what we've discovered." He drew closer. "I wouldn't have asked anyone else, and I haven't."

I studied his look of desperation in his steady eyes, and the solemn glance was trustworthy. So I agreed. We exchanged a firm handshake, and then it was back to my yacht for the night. Ahmed left in his silvery *Mercedes-Benz* and his State escort of several cars with Egyptian national flags on their radio antennae.

January 20, 2011: Late Morning

Nile Port of Memphis, near Cairo

Arrival in Memphis took the remainder of yesterday and most of the night. Thankful for a strong wind, we made it. I was reminded to cover up, both for native religious concerns and because I sunburn easily. I packed some *Aloe Vera* in the shoulder bag I was to wear, and some excavation tools. My servant handed me a canteen of mineral water, which I gracefully accepted.

At the port I decided to 'go native' and ride a Camel, for the purchasing price of *Baksheesh* (local tips, or customary bribes) in the way of a half-dozen blank USB Drives. Madame Julia remained on board the *Athena*.

An hour later I arrived in Saqqara. The seasonal traffic seemed closer to Cairo for some unclear reason. The site was bustling with activity of an archaeological nature. People carried chunks of rocks and dirt to be screened in large metal frames, looking for precious artifacts. Some poured water into them to soften the rocks. Others knelt in the dust with brushes. Some hacked the stone fence with chisels and hammers, picks and mallets. A tractor or some vehicle hauled away excess stone, clearing the path. And surveyors photographed everything with digital 35MM Cameras.

"Ahmed!" I called out to the man in the relaxed gray sports coat and cool sunglasses. He responded with a wave of one free hand, and a simple smile.

"Doctor Costa," he started. "I have some friends for you to meet. Omar, this is Dr. M. J. Costa, CEO of the *Taharqa Institute of Ancient Languages*. Dr. Costa has supplied us with some data on our discovery here in Saqqara."

After greeting me with the usual Arabic, Omar Al-Masri, Head of the *Oriental Institute of Archaeology*, handed me a digital display of the structure below us. The blue 3D diagram showed no openings on the four sides of this building, but it did show several side rooms and a cavity to the north. He pointed out the shaft leading to a well of some sort.

My data was the translation of faint glyphs seen by the satellite photos, just below a layer of silt on the floor of the excavation site. Omar asked about this.

"So Doctor, our satellites managed to find these glyphs? Where do they lead?" Omar asked.

In pointing out the location, we walked toward the upper edge of the buried structure. The excavators cleaned the stone floor so that the edges were visible. One plastered-over triangle was exposed when I leaned against it, causing the plaster to crumble.

"I wasn't expecting that! Ahmed, over here, I found something," I said.

Ahmed came running. "You found - ah, a triangle! Praise to God," he said.

The triangle, now cleaned with a set of old toothbrushes and some baby oil, was a right-triangle glyph. It had a recess of four centimeters. I showed Omar this.

"You mean, it, it's a button?" He asked me.

"Yes," I replied. "You just press on it, like this," I replied while handling the triangle and clamping it to its base. A stone-on-stone sound was heard below our feet. A minute of silence was followed by an artificial earthquake of some kind, then the sound of rushing water.

"Dr. Costa, I must tell you something you may have missed in Archaeology school," Ahmed replied. "Do you remember the old films about tombs with curses and traps?"

"Ah yes?" I asked.

"Well, this is one of them. *Mind your head*," he said.

I looked around me. The rock walls started to loosen and the stone floor gave way. I fell through an opening just below the triangle and into a pool.

Omar fell in with me. Ahmed had enough sense to jump backwards. The room was dark until some ceiling rocks collapsed. Behind me were a waterfall and a statue of a Cat god. I took a minute to adjust to the dimness of my environment.

Ahmed wondered, "Dr. Costa, *do you see anything*?"

"Yes," I replied. "*Wonderful things* - I wish."

Ahmed laughed a bit at the reference. He tossed down a rope and two large flash lights. I tossed one to Omar.

The floor was wet with tepid water and limestone. We walked about a quarter mile in this cave. We found nothing of interest. Well except for two similar triangles. I studied one up close.

The triangle had a strange, Scarab shape protruding from its center. The other one was a Ma'at feather. The room was a solid wall in all directions, except for the waterfall and its pool. Wait. "Omar, what was in that pool back there?" I asked.

Omar jogged back to the entrance. "It's a golden bug. A Scarab, I think. Why?"

"Press it," I ordered.

"If you insist," he replied. The triangle lit up a bright green on the Scarab shape. Rocks started to crumble along the upper edges of the room. Then I saw why.

"Omar! Look up!" I announced.

"What?" he asked in hesitation.

"The glyphs from the satellite map are below the rocks. Do you remember what they were?" I asked.

Omar winced a bit. Then he rummaged his pockets looking for answers, finding a folded paper of interest. Unfolding it, he quickly read the top translation from the Greek or Demotic dialect.

The rocks fell into the room, mixing with the waterfall and revealed golden letters in ancient glyphs. The glyphs seemed to read right to left, and left to right, but they stopped in the middle of the room where a single glyph was placed.

"Bast!" I said aloud. "It's Bast! The words point to Bast the Cat Goddess!"

"Where?" Omar added. Omar looked around himself.

The lineup of glyphs was uncanny. The glyph for Bast was not in profile, and was unusual for Egyptian languages that mostly favored profiles. Below this glyph was a string of letters leading to a fourth triangle.

"Okay, that was interesting," I said. "I wonder..."

Omar asked, "What about *this* triangle? The one with the *Emerald* Eye, which I believe has a small indentation for a shape of some sort. Yes, it's a cat."

"A Cat? Let me look," I said. The hole had a cat image with emeralds for eyes. But this image was hollow, as if missing a component. Then I remembered the amulet about my neck. I was right. It was the same shape. I removed it from my neck and inserted it into the space where it resonated with a simple click.

"Now what?" Omar asked me.

"Ah, press it?" I replied. "Good. A click." I played around with the switch and nothing happened. Omar leaned back against the wall as I tried to decipher the ceiling glyphs. Then I heard a stone grinding sound behind me. The wall with the triangle opened as I fell backwards, sliding down a few stone steps. Omar gathered his senses with the flashlight sending much needed illumination in my direction. "Damn water traps!"

We descended the stone staircase as it winded for a quarter mile into darkness. The walls were plain sandstone with no ornamentation. Was this a tomb or another trap? We entered a clearing. Four stone squares stood alone in the center of the room. A golden cat statue lay in the background. Omar thought it was safe to cross, but I was wiser.

I grabbed a small pebble from the walkway and cast it onto the stone floor with the loose tiles before us.

The pebble landed on a small square of loose stone. The stone sank into its recess. Then the walls started to change. One wall glyph, an Eye shape, started to leak fine yellow sand. The sand was not the problem. The real problem was the fact the sand was the result of walls closing in onto us, as if released by some ancient hydraulics system. Then the walls stopped, and the stone panel popped back up, and returned to their former state.

"It's a primitive *spring* of some kind," Omar deduced.

As we studied the ancient puzzle I noticed a cat walked past us and onto the stone grid. I tried to scoot it away with a stick so it wouldn't activate the trap. It stood its ground, looked at us and meowed.

We exchanged glances.

An hour later, after we lured the cat over here with a piece of Sushi, we convinced it to carry the amulet about its neck and activate the panel in the far wall. The wall panel was in the shape of a cat, and the amulet was magnetically attracted to it, clinging to it. I influenced the cat with my laser pointer. Cats just *love* colored lights.

The trap was *ingenious*, so the reward *must* be great. Or so we believed.

I opened the wall panel with a *Swiss Army Knife* I kept in my utility jacket. No pressing anything this time. Omar agreed.

The wall before us slid open with a robust tug along some ancient hinge. We walked on ahead. I cautioned Omar when we encountered what appeared to be a tripwire of some kind. A hole in the ceiling directly above us and one of two in front of us gave me suspicion.

"I just hope it's not a rock," I said candidly.

"There's only one way to know," Omar said as he cut the rope tripwire with the knife blade. A sound was heard above. This one was different.

"Do you hear that?" I asked him.

"Yes. It sounds like mechanical, not stone. Would it be...?"

I pushed him aside as this device fell onto us from above. It was a spinning top made of gold. The only problem here was that it held four very sharp blades on each face.

"You recall the chariot spokes of Darius during the Battle of Issus?" I asked Omar. Omar glanced at me with contempt. We both dove to the floor, and ran back to the entrance. The top spun about until it exhausted its forward momentum. "There. All done," I replied.

Omar walked over to inspect the gold top, and I felt a sudden pain in my ears. It was a ringing sound followed by a lapse of consciousness. A voice commanded me in some archaic dialect not heard in millennium. Then images haunted me. Yes, images are a form of language, one that precedes vocabulary. The voice then spoke to me in a form of English, almost like a whisper at first, then as a command.

"I Am...Bast. Bast! I Command You, Mortal, fleshling! Bring me the Emerald Scarab. Bring me my sustenance for my Shabtis, O Ka of Bast, she who commands you, Obey!" the voice announced in my head.

Omar examined the golden rope on the spin top then saw me double over.

"Doctor! Are you well?" Omar asked.

I uncovered my ears. "Yes?" I asked.

"I saw you there, for a moment, I thought."

"Omar, are there any giant emerald scarabs near the two holes in front of us?" I asked in desperation.

"I don't know. I'll go look..." Omar walked over to the holes. "How large a scarab?"

"It doesn't matter," I said. "Anything."

He dropped a light stick down the first hole. It bounced off a small jewel in the limelight. He knelt down a bit.

"Yes," he smiled. "Come over here."

I walked over to the hole. The light stick was lying next to a gold-encrusted emerald. "I could buy a new yacht with that rock," I replied.

I lowered myself down the hole. It was about a two meter drop. The scarab was finely carved. The encrustation was seemingly modern, in the shape of a lotus flower with a row of glyphs on the underside and a cat glyph at both ends. The emerald was the size of a ML baseball.

The next hole had something else to discover. Omar walked over to it.

"Dr. Costa, we have stairs," he said smiling.

The stairs led to a crypt with golden walls. Finely engraved glyphs were embedded in the gold walls, and led to the double door with iron hinges and bolts. A thin rope was sealed with a clay lock, stamped with the *Seal of Anubis*, a standard necropolis seal for a tomb.

We exchanged smiles.

I withdrew my *Swiss Army Knife* and cut the delicate rope to open it. I slid open the bolts with ease. The hinges took a few pulls to open. Inside a burst of air shot out. Then the scent of flowers overpowered us. A few minutes later, I entered slowly, my flashlight beaming ahead of me.

An array of features presented themselves in my light. Foreign shapes, statues, and golden trinkets were bundled together like military tribute given to a conqueror. A solid gold bowl with dried meat lay undisturbed near the front. Three water libation vessels of silver stood nearby. A faience cup lay on its side.

Then I approached a golden mummy case in the shape of a feline goddess, surrounded by four statues of cats. One was Mafdet, another was Sakhmet. The two others were Tefnut and Bast. Four Canopic jars were found a short distance away with cat stoppers on their tops. Omar opened one and found it contained shriveled up grain, not bodily organs as expected. He opened the remaining three.

"What are these for? Corn, barley, and Catnip! This isn't a tomb. These are not lungs or kidneys. The body must have been interred whole..." Omar stopped.

The golden mummy case lid was heavy, so I removed the locks on its edge. Then we raised it with a crowbar from my shoulder pack. The case lid had hinges along one edge. "How thoughtful," I remarked.

Under the case lid was a linen shroud with a flower garland around the top. "Mandrakes, lilies, and roses," Omar said. I photographed this with my digital camera.

Omar removed the shroud. Then we saw it.

"It's.. . a woman. Wait. There's no mummy here! It's a woman sleeping in this, this gel. We must remove her before she drowns," Omar said in fear.

The gel was a form of suspended animation. Instinctively I reached for the emerald scarab. Then I placed it over her head, waiting for a reaction.

"Hmm... nothing. Is this the correct mummy case?" I asked the silence of the room.

"Maybe if you read it, just saying," Omar replied.

"Okay," I started. "My translation, 'Behold the rising of Sothis, the light of Ra in Nut, come, take up your child and bask in its light. I call forth, you, who are hidden in truth, come, open up your wings and breathe life into the Daughter of the Sun, Bast, the Goddess of Cats.'"

The woman in the gel below us pushed her head up and inhaled heavily, her eyes still closed. Our initial shock wore off after her Caucasian complexion with the cat tattoos and knotted brown hair awoke to modern day technology. Omar's cell phone was ringing. It was Ahmed, he wanted an update.

"Ah a cat with real green eyes," I said to the woman in the gel, as she shivered. "Omar, your jacket." He handed me his jacket so I could dress the woman in something warm. The desert air had not yet entered this room. "Hmm.. your hairspray gel, your highness," I told the woman as we lifted her up from her mummy case. She didn't say a word, not that I would be able to answer her anyway.

An hour later, we escorted the woman up the main room where the waterfall is. Ahmed had sent a rope ladder down with a paramedic bringing us some supplies and clothing. We had her checked out. Vitals were somewhat normal, AB+ blood type, no rabies or cat-bites thankfully. She drank a full carton of milk, and seemed to know to remember how to eat, though carefully prepared Sushi helped somewhat. Her blood sample was sent to a local laboratory for analysis; not that we didn't trust where exactly it came from. She had a full physical exam, then a mental one, though English seemed a bit illogical in my opinion, outside of that headache down there. Then I remembered the Emerald Scarab.

As the doctors tried to communicate with her, I remembered the linen wrapping from the Bast amulet. The photo was still on my cell phone. It was a name: **Bast-en-ka-nefer, High Priestess of Bast**. It matched the amulet's cartouche. I took out the amulet and dangled it in front of her, you know, to jog her memory. She saw this and was mesmerized. Then she smiled broadly.

"Bast! Bast-en-ka-nefer!" She pointed at the amulet then to her chest. Then she started rambling in a dialect of Near Eastern gibberish. I alerted Julia on my cell phone. Julia is a Coptic Christian. Copts speak in Ancient Egyptian dialect. Though the cell phone was unusual, the woman heard Coptic on one end and spoke excitedly into it as Julia communicated with her for an hour.

I asked Ahmed if it was okay for me to assist the woman on our yacht, to which he responded as if I took his prize away and wanted to keep it. But then he relented, saying it was my priority to learn about this mystery woman. So now Bast is on our yacht, learning modern culture and how to speak in English, French, and Arabic via our digital translator from our company. Okay, so it's a robot. But it works.

I let the woman keep the amulet. She wears it every night. The Emerald Scarab is in the Cairo Museum on display. The tomb is still being excavated, and its treasures are under tight security. We adopted the mysterious Cat, and it likes the laser pointer and ancient Catnip I found.

Sunday, January 23, 2011: Evening

At the Cairo City Museum, Upper Floor

Our Ancient friend settled in my yacht quite nicely, so I thought it appropriate to give her an after-hours guided tour of the Cairo Museum. She, as her description merited, is a High Priestess of the Cat Goddess Bast. She lived in the 22nd Dynasty according to the trappings in her converted tomb. As to why she was placed in the suspended animation gel, there are still unanswered questions. The gel is undergoing tests in the Cairo laboratory. I should have answers by next week.

Julia created a Coptic-English translation device to be worn on Bast's belt. This will automatically translate everything she says, with voice-recognition and activated technology from my company. We have a production studio on board the *Athena*. We came prepared, as usual.

While exploring the Cairo Museum upstairs, Bast noticed the obvious collection of the *Golden Pharaoh*. She saw something of interest, and asked a Museum Staff member about it. It was a silver trumpet.

"Why yes, it's the *Tut-ankh-Amon* trumpet. We only have two of them," the Staff member replied.

"May I look closer?" Bast asked honestly.

"Well, I guess no harm can come from it. Of course, just let me open the glass panel and disable the security features..."

Bast handled the trumpet. She asked the Staff member to try blowing into it, as it seemed a bit tarnished. As he did this, Bast noticed something familiar about the design. The sound echoed in the room, and vibrations bounced off the golden chariot in the next display case. Bast backed up a few feet, with a strange feeling of dread. The golden Canopic Chest on display behind her had an inscription she recognized.

"No! NOO!" she exclaimed.

The Staff member replaced the silver trumpet back into its display case, and then asked her about her outburst.

"It's Isfet! Isfet is coming out! We must leave," She said hysterically.

"Who is Isfet?" the Staff member asked her.

"*Isfet is the Egyptian word for injustice or violence*," said the translator.

"We *must* go. Doctor Costa, I can't remain in this building. We must return to your boat," Bast instructed. "A great evil is coming."

"Don't you want to see our latest exhibit? It's an *emerald scarab*," I said.

"You don't understand, we --," she stopped. "You have an emerald scarab?"

"Yes. I forgot to show you earlier. I found it with your mummy case," I replied. She frowned and approached me.

"*You* entered and defiled the Sanctuary of Bast? *Where* is the Scarab?" she demanded. I pointed towards her right hand. A locked display case was visible. She noticed it, and then said something illegible to my modern ears.

The lights in the Museum fluctuated and flickered violently. A computer behind me *Crashed To Desktop*, and a few security cameras stopped working. Then a fierce wind entered the Museum from nowhere, as all the windows were secured. Bast pointed to the display case, and it unlocked itself. Then it opened. Bast saw me watch her in disbelief, and picked up the *emerald scarab* and held it to her breast. She turned it upside-down and opened a hidden door I must have overlooked. Inside it was a small glass vial. She opened it and then drank the contents. For a moment she appeared nauseated. Then it happened. The voice in my head returned. I blacked out for a minute, clinging to my ears. When I awoke I saw something different.

A golden-skinned figure stood before me. Her head was a lioness with sparkling, emerald green eyes and rich golden fur covering her mane. Her neck was bejeweled with golden collars adorned with gemstones in the shape of hieroglyphs. A snake crown decorated her hair, also made of gold and gems. She wore a green gown of an unknown fabric that tapered to her body like silk, with a slit for her muscled calves. Her finger and toe nails appeared as lion claws. A single word penetrated my cranium - "BAST."

A small dust storm appeared at her feet, and encircled her. When it reached her neck, she smiled for some reason and then disappeared into the swirling dust. The voice returned to my ears, this time I fainted.

I awoke on the morning of January 25, 2011 in a hospital bed. I was not on my yacht. Julia was at my bedside, with a worried servant looking on. She handed me a newspaper. Apparently there was a new political revolution in Egypt, one that had nurtured itself in nearby Tunisia. The doctor said I was unconscious for several hours.

"Where is Bast?" I asked.

"We don't know," Julia related. "But we have an idea."

In *Tahrir Square*, a large crowd of tumultuous people gathered to listen to a brown-haired woman dressed in strange clothing. She stood atop a sphinx statue, and her voice carried via a microphone that led to an Internet port. It was Bast.

"Do you want to continue the injustice you suffered under the military dictatorship? Do you like being poor, with no economic oversight, where high officials accept bribes?" Bast asked the people who responded with cheers of support. "Today, millennium of history look upon you, for justice is at hand!"

"Down with the dictator! Down with the *Pharaoh*!" cried the people.

"Hmm, *Pharaoh*? Ah, you mean *him*," She said as she witnessed the crowd burn a photo of the reigning President.

"Freedom! We want Freedom, Liberty! We want *money*!"

"I can offer you all this, and more. Pledge your loyalty to me, and I will grant you the freedom to choose your own President, to choose your own religion, and to keep your family safe from the secret police! And by joining me, your emergency laws will end," Bast promised.

"Why should we trust you?" asked one female onlooker.

"Because I represent your history," Bast started. "A beautiful history, one that never really ended. . . One which is now unfolding, one which shall be reborn! Come, join me, Lady Bast!" Bast announced this while channeling her inner nature into the Internet website and through the loudspeakers.

"Who is that woman?" asked the Chief of Police inside the Presidential Palace in Cairo. "She doesn't appear to be any citizen I ever encountered. She must be foreign!"

"What should we do?" asked the President's Chief of Staff.

"Cut the Internet. Stop the electricity. And one more thing. . . Release the Prisoners. This shall put an end to her machinations," the President ordered.

Then as Bast was about to entertain the people with her plans, the loudspeakers suddenly went dead. The Internet services were cut. The people reacted with anger, but not against Bast. They took the message into the streets.

Bast lost all control over this riot. Her hopes of winning over people to do her bidding seemed to have ended, for now. Frowning, she climbed down from the sphinx statue and mixed into the moving crowd as they marched to the Presidential Palace and the Cairo Museum. The riot became violent. Some people smashed glass windows, threw rocks and incendiary devices, and damaged cars with pieces of metal.

Back in the Hospital, I was informed my seizure was not normal, and all other tests returned negative. Bast must use a form of mind control. Ahmed called my cell phone and left a message. The tests on Bast's blood sample contained interesting information. I took a few pain-killer medicines and exited the Hospital an hour or so later and played back the message.

"Dr. Costa, it's Ahmed... The blood sample from Bast indicates an unusual peak of energy-containing platelets. We think this is caused by the *Emerald Scarab* or some ancient radiation. The same radiation emits from KV62 when a Geiger counter is applied. We last found her on local television and on a social network, trying to encourage the natives to overthrow the Egyptian Government following the fall of Tunisia a few days ago. Now that the Government has cut off the Internet and electricity grid, we think she is on her way back to her tomb in Saqqara. As is, the only place she can call a sanctuary is in that place. I will join you there in an hour..."

I returned to my docked yacht via an escort as the main city of Cairo was, well, busy... Traffic congestion was immense, owing to the Revolution. Rows of armed police blocked intersections and the Army was called in to repress the rowdy groups of "peaceful" protesters. Some protesters were armed with primitive weapons despite attempts to carry nothing; anarchists apparently like riots and flock to the occasion.

Our yacht suffered no damage since we removed the national flag and lowered our American flag halfway. My Servant readied the modified Jet-ski (the one with hidden devices) and assembled my adventure garb. There was a slight breeze in the air, with a heavy scent of pollutants or fire coming from Cairo to the north. One can only guess why.

The excavation site was unusually vacant today. There was a formal steel ladder leading into the bottom level near the crypt. The surrounding areas where archaeologists sifted clay from artifacts was off limits; four canisters full of artifacts stood on the foreground. Ahmed's car was seen in the distance.

"Doctor Costa! Come on down," Ahmed announced. "And bring a helmet. The cave is slowly deteriorating."

Descending the steel ladder was easier than the initial fall. With a fiberglass hardhat on, I entered the antechamber with Ahmed's flashlight bouncing off the decaying limestone. A recent rain had softened the ancient stone foundation into a mix of gypsum, water and lime. The original glyphs along the upper edge still exist, but the Bast images seemed a bit tarnished.

"Where was her last location, Doctor?" Ahmed asked.

"In Cairo," I started. "There's a political rally there."

"Well, not to worry... I am no politician. Politics and Archaeology never really mix. We excavate, that's about it. We *preserve* History, we don't *make* it. Now with Bast here, maybe things will change. Maybe..."

A scream was heard that interrupted Ahmed and excited me. I switched on my battery operated flashlight and started to carefully sprint to the location of the scream. Ahmed followed.

Another scream was heard to the East. I pointed in that direction and decided to corner to the West. Ahmed approached the tomb, crowbar in hand. Then something came out. It was a leopard. Ahmed yelled in anticipation.

"Hold still!" I shouted. "I will lasso it with the rope."

The leopard turned its spotted head and focused its sparkling green eyes into my gaze. Then it leapt onto me. I noticed a translation belt attached to a flea collar along its neck. The leopard threatened me with its claws, until I read the inscription I remembered from the *Emerald Scarab.* A burning bright yellow light followed by a puff of white smoke enveloped the leopard. A second later, the leopard was replaced by a woman with brown hair and strong fingers that clawed at my face. While staring into her eyes, I twisted one wrist and broke her grasp. Her eyes then narrowed in anger, and she backed off.

"Sacrilege! You defiled my Sanctuary with impudence!" Bast proclaimed in anger. She stood up and dressed herself in a slim wetsuit that had been lying on the ground.

"We have something that belongs to you," Ahmed waved the *Emerald Scarab* with his free hand.

"The Scarab! Oh. . . I am honored," Bast calmed herself. "I still need to study its effects."

"What effects?" I asked with a heavy breath.

Bast turned to me. "I originally found this *Emerald Scarab* in a tomb not far from here. It belonged to the *Emerald Pharaoh*. My history was replete with references to a Pharaoh that cheated death, or lived forever, by a certain green stone. It may even be *this one*."

"So... You're saying this *Emerald Pharaoh* was immortal?" Ahmed inquired.

"No. He was mortal. But he lived for 200 years," Bast replied.

"Why did he die then?" I asked.

"In my opinion, he was alone. All his family and close friends had since perished during the first 100 years. Immortality was not seen as valuable to him if he could not share it with someone. So he gave up his immortality by placing the *Emerald Scarab* in a Temple or Sanctuary, and later died a normal death some 10 days later," Bast explained.

"Do you remember his name?" Ahmed asked.

"Yes. It was Psosis or Psamtik. Yes, it was S-ankh-ra Psamtik," Bast replied.

"Hmm... I will run it through our database. Doctor, you should bring Bast back to your yacht. I will tidy up the tomb here, in case of rats attracted to the dampness," Ahmed said.

"Oh rats? There are no rats in here," Bast replied. "At least there were no rats since lunch." Bast smiled slyly.

On the surface we walked along the rocky path to Ahmed's *Mercedes* car while he texted on his cell phone to the SCA. Some seven minutes passed. I exchanged glances with Bast frequently. She had been braiding her hair while wearing a simple T-Shirt and wetsuit with *Romanesque* sandals. Ahmed looked up from his cell phone, and smirked slightly.

"Doctor Costa, I know where to find Psamtik's tomb. It's in a local cemetery," Ahmed said. "I'm positive the locals won't mind us excavating there."

"Why is that? The gods would never approve," Bast said.

Ahmed turned. "The locals are in Cairo, and the cemetery is deserted."

"We should prepare an offering," Bast added. "It will ensure good fortune."

"I am not bringing any bread," I said. "My physician is against added *Carbohydrates*."

"No, no, of course not. I am Bast, not Osiris. We can offer some fruits or chickpeas mixed with a fish offering. We can find some in there," she said while pointing towards the Nile River.

We passed by a local merchant stand. It had everything we required for the offering. I placed a few hundred pound notes in the donation box for compensation. The merchant was not available, obviously.

We arrived in the decadent cemetery by 1pm. Numerous headstones, mostly fallen into ruin, decorated the coarse ground and sparse grasses. A slim stone joint protruded from some caked earth in the back area. In front of this were a stone pillar, a step, and two tombstones dating back to 1800's CE. Some excavation equipment was to be found nearby. Apparently illegal excavations started all over Egypt during the riots in Cairo. I asked Ahmed about this.

"Yes, I have heard about them. Criminals, vandals, thieves! That ruffian appears throughout our history, mostly during economic hardship. Here, hand me that shovel and the crowbar. We're going inside," Ahmed said.

Ahmed raised the crowbar up and let it hit the stone step before us. It wasn't a real stone step, but a cover for a man hole that led underground. We looked at each other, and then descended the integrated metal rungs.

"I used to travel down here as a child. It's called the Saqqaran Catacombs. No one knows who built them, probably during the Late Period in my opinion. I once found a tomb filled with alabaster Shabtis, until some merchant in the Cairo Bazaar sold them as souvenirs to tourists," Ahmed said while we walked inside a concrete or stone tunnel.

"Remarkable," Bast said.

"Yes, but the sad part is these ruins will never see the light of day. What you are walking on is protected property of the Egyptian Government. Or what Americans call a nuclear silo. So naturally all these tombs here are vandal fodder now," Ahmed explained.

"That would explain the radiation," I stated while activating a Geiger counter. Then I placed it near Bast and received some indications.

"Will you stop it?" she said in defense.

"Gods must be radioactive," I told her.

"It's called *Power*," she replied. "Go back to *Sunday school.*"

We approached a clearing. Ahmed motioned to us to halt. My Geiger counter had unusual readings around a blank wall. The stone Masonry was excellent except for a rectangular recess along an edge in front. I banged on it lightly with my fist. It was hollow.

"Allow me?" Bast asked as she kicked down the wall with a forward thrust. Inside this passageway was more stone brick architecture. This led for about a minute until we found a sealed chamber. Two granite sphinxes guarded a stone block for a doorway. On the surface was a double Cartouche.

"S-Ankh-Ra Psamtik, Lord of the Two Lands, who lives for millions of years," I read from the inscription.

"Is anyone home?" Bast asked.

Ahmed blasted his flashlight onto the stone plug, looking for a niche or button. He found a crevice in the shape of a dung beetle.

"I see. It wants the Scarab," Bast said as she inserted the *Emerald Scarab* into the crevice. It entered slowly, and then she turned it clockwise and unlocked the stone plug. The stone plug descended into the floor with a stone-on-stone sound.

"There must be a pulley or some kind of hydraulics, but I don't see any," Ahmed said. He switched on his flashlight into the tomb.

"Ahh," Ahmed smiled. "Psamtik!"

There before us was a solid silver mummy case with emeralds and malachite stones decorating the lid. Emerald mines existed in Egypt during the Ptolemy Dynasty. Before then, only malachite was known. Certain green stones contained ancient powers, or so related the priests.

"Even the eyes have emeralds!" I said. "And look! Hinges."

"The SCA would have my arm if they found this out," Ahmed replied in excitement. "Though the radiation would prevent tourism, it seems."

"No, the only radiation here is coming from the *Emerald Scarab* and of course, Bast," I said while using the counter.

"Not yet," Ahmed said. "Hand me that crowbar."

We inserted the crowbar into the hinged lid and applied pressure until it opened. Some gases seeped from the metal coffin, as usual. The mummy was not well preserved, if at all. The skeletal corpse was clutching a roll of papyrus sealed in wax. Other features included amulets and talismans of varied jewels, gemstones, and glass beads. The skeleton was also draped in a solid gold outfit of some kind, with a gold-beaded skull cap. The papyrus was of especial interest to me, as a linguist.

Ahmed photographed everything to preserve the original positions of the items. Illegal excavators would not, of course, care to do that.

"These are for the SCA if we can convince them to visit this place," Ahmed said. "I'll hand you the papyrus for translation in a bit. No one wanted this man to live forever, or any longer. I wonder if this was his last wish?"

As Ahmed pried the papyrus from Psamtik's grasp, something happened. A shrill of some kind emitted from the tomb. Bast instinctively knelt before it in ancient homage, then remembered something and started to gather together fruits and flowers. Ahmed and I covered our ears. A loud voice boomed in Coptic language and transferred into Bast's translator on her belt.

"Hold Intruder! Do not commit sacrilege against the Son of Ra! Go back unto your homeland, or the wrath of Sakhemet is before you..." announced the disembodied voice of Psamtik.

Psamtik's corpse rose from the coffin, his mummy still with its arms crossed. Three emeralds triangulated to form a light face, which sent a fireball in our direction, several times. As this was happening, Bast placed a wreath of flowers and fruits on the base of the coffin.

"The offering! It must be seen!" Bast cried. Then she added a freshly caught fish to the pile. She looked up then smirked. "You want *incense*, O

Pharaoh?" She tossed up some Cedar Incense into the air and a fireball struck it, causing the incense to explode into wafts of scented smoke. This scent found its way into the coffin. Then without warning everything stopped. The corpse fell back into the coffin and the fireballs were extinguished.

"Bast, you did it. Now we can. . . Doctor Costa!" Ahmed said.

While Bast was offering to the corpse of Psamtik, the Ka Spirit of the Pharaoh had entered my body. My behavior now was that of a reincarnated Egyptian King. My eyes were dilated and my voice was a whisper. The Ka Spirit left the corpse of Psamtik and this caused the corpse to collapse, not the incense.

"Hand me the Book," Psamtik said via my voice.

Ahmed stared at me in disbelief. Bast was not convinced.

"Here is the papyrus, just don't hurt anyone," Ahmed said.

I received the papyrus and opened the seal, then started to read it aloud in Ancient Egyptian Demotic script. Bast's translator helped with the English version, and Ahmed learned the secrets of the *Emerald Scarab*. Bast approached me with the *Emerald Scarab* in her left hand, and then slapped me with her right.

"Awaken, Doctor Costa. It's only a dream life," She said as she stared into my eyes. A moment later I dropped to my knees, and the papyrus roll fell to the ground. A bright golden light appeared on the ceiling, and then vanished outside.

I reached for the papyrus, but Bast stood one foot on my hand in prevention. I looked up. She had her arms folded with an angry look on her face.

"Haven't you done enough desecration for one day?" she asked me.

"What was all that?" Ahmed interjected.

"That," Bast replied, "Was Psamtik."

"Oh," Ahmed and I said in unison.

"We must find his disembodied Ka Spirit before he causes some mischief. It seems he has a yearning for wealth, judging by the contents of this room. Silver was valued higher than commonplace gold in our day. Where does one put wealth today?" Bast asked.

"In a bank," Ahmed replied. "There's one main branch in Alexandria. I think it's the *Bank of Cheops*. I know of two local branches. One is in Cairo. The other is ..."

"Bast, is Psamtik the Isfet?" I asked her.

"Doctor, Isfet is everywhere now. I would not accept it was confined to one person alone. There is no living personification," She said in a meditative tone.

Ahmed searched his cell phone database. The backup generator on board my yacht has a separate satellite connection with dish. As Cairo is suffering from lack of electricity and all satellites are offline, this helps our situation. Ahmed found something.

"Ah of course! The local branch of the Bank of Cheops is in Giza!"

"The Great Pyramid?" Bast echoed.

"No. It's below that," Ahmed replied. "But you may be onto something."

Bast picked up the papyrus scroll and examined it somewhat. Then she unrolled it partway and read a few lines in Coptic. Her eyes remembered something, a flash back of ancient knowledge. She saw a boat in the midst of a freely flowing Nile River. On the boat were three men. One wore a shoulder cloth and carried a papyrus scepter; he must be a priest. Another was a sailor, judging by the fact he held the rudder of the boat. The third wore a blue and gold striped head cloth, and was well adorned with jewelry. "Pharaoh," Bast said to her vision. The Pharaoh held an *Emerald Scarab* up to the sky. The clouds parted and divine light descended before him, opening a portal of some kind. Out of the portal was a golden apple. Pharaoh reached for the apple and took it, bit into it, and replaced the apple into the portal. Then the vision stopped and Bast could see nothing else.

"Bast? Bast are you coming?" Ahmed asked her once the vision ended.

Bast closed her eyes a moment then regained her senses.

January 26, 2011

Port of Giza, Near the Great Pyramid

1:34pm

The cool breeze calmed a stifled sneeze after two camels had donated their dung to the city landscape. Then one turned its lengthy neck my direction while chewing on local grasses and belched; the scent of mulch became memorable.

Ahmed had visited Cairo earlier today for some assistance. He was met by some protesters demanding jobs at the SCA. Archaeology jobs had peaked prior to the Revolution and following the demotion of a popular Egyptologist during one of the riots. But there was no one with enough doctorates to fill the positions. Someone trained natives with Egyptology; so much for Asian child labor laws.

Ahmed's people included a female military trainer, four former soldiers, an accountant, a conservator, and six laborers. He introduced each one.

"Good. So let's go then?" I asked him.

Across the way someone was walking with a black briefcase, and wore a black suit with bow tie and a top hat. Now *no one* wears black suits with top hats in the heat of Egypt. The figure entered the *Bank of Cheops*, as we watched from a distance.

"Ahmed, assemble your people. We're going in," I alerted Ahmed.

Inside the bank people busily cashed overdue checks, made deposits, and added to their savings. Some gambled on the stock market despite the Revolution in Cairo. Backup generators supplied electricity with the solar panels on the east side of the Great Pyramid nearby. The figure in black managed to elude the security camera and entered the adjoining bathroom. Inside one empty stall, the figure removed his overcoat, gloves, and hat. He opened the briefcase and removed a small silvery device, in the shape of an Orb.

Security guards were alerted by Ahmed's people. The bathroom was secured from all activity, as soldiers used ropes to prevent movement inside. A small silvery spider, resembling an Orb weaver, scuttled below everyone's feet as the group slowly entered the bathroom. One soldier poked his semi-automatic rifle into each stall, claiming it from the mysterious figure's reach. The last stall was there before us. We approached carefully. Then we noticed something peculiar. The man inside was unconscious, and sat atop the toilet seat.

"What the--," stopped one soldier.

"How is he unconscious? Did we do this?" asked Ahmed in frustration.

Ahmed ordered the man's body vacated from the bank. Some paramedics entered and secured the man to a white transport bed. No one entered and no one left. How did Psamtik avoid security?

Outside the bathroom, the silvery Orb weaver "spider" scuttled onto a bank desk by jumping from the carpeted floor. It moved quickly. One item caught its attention: the computer system. Every bank is computerized. They all have the same access, the same files format that controls the numbers secured by the bank. The spider stood over the computer security device and started typing random words and phrases. It was searching for a pass code. The bank uses a universal bank pass code to access State funds. Of particular interest was the code of the Swiss Bank accounts that most dictators adored. This one had about $340 Billion Pounds in it. The spider sent this amount to an undisclosed location, then scurried away as Ahmed and his people entered the bank.

"So you say, the security guards never entered or left?" Ahmed spoke into his cell phone. "What was the man in black doing in here in the first place?"

"He left a briefcase, sir," said the Accountant. "You might want to see this, sir."

Ahmed turned about, his behavior bordering on rage. Then he saw the blueprints inside the briefcase. "By the grace of God!"

"Doctor Costa, it's Ahmed," Ahmed said on his radio as I entered the room. He saw me then beamed his right index finger to the blueprints, *My Blueprints*!

I examined the blueprints with earnest. It was an earlier design for a robot army, one that I never continued due to cost. The point was I did not have enough storage space, and it used up my reserve of costly titanium plate for the prototypes. This one was slightly altered and beset with armaments of a foreign company. I do recall having the originals shredded, so this one was probably a copy, or so I told Ahmed.

I asked him if he saw anything out of the ordinary in the room with the man. "No, nothing. I even checked the latrine," he told me.

"So now a mystery has our designs. And that mystery is a disembodied Ka Spirit of an Ancient Egyptian King with sights on conquering the known world with a robot army?" I asked. "Don't look at me. Go get my popcorn!"

January 29, 2011

During the Cairo Riots in Cairo, Egypt

3:34 pm

For the past 3 days, we scoured the city and country searching for any sign of Psamtik. The only evidence for a robot army was a transmission to a site in Northern Iran. It seems they were producing *something* there. The USA Spy Satellites helped with our investigation.

Ahmed returned to the SCA for maintenance and to prevent looting from the Cairo Museum. I was back on my yacht with Julia and Bast. The maintenance bill finally arrived via email. The Egyptian Government restored *some* Internet traffic, mostly for *their* use. The Israeli Consulate was recently invaded by protesters. Two important documents went missing. One concerned itself with nuclear weapons technology. The other contained detailed information regarding clothing fashion of the early British Occupation of Egypt, post-Napoleonic era.

The Cairo Museum had a recent theft. People who entered it were idiots, because they stole statues from KV62, the well-documented ones that are gold-plated wood and not solid gold as everyone knows. They are also idiots because of the items' former owner. Nothing *really* valuable was missing. They can't sell damaged goods, even on a black market.

Bast explored the wondrous modern Cosmetics available in a local **Giza** merchant shop. We decided to visit it following the incident in the silo. She never noticed glittery nail polish would go well with henna tattoos. I offered to play a game of *Hounds and Jackals* with her, but she cried it was too commonplace for a woman of her stature. She instead became transfixed by online computer games like *World of Egypt* (WOE), or online *Strip Poker*.

Outside during the riots someone saw a UFO hovering. Perhaps it was Psamtik spying on us, or a real one. Or possibly it was a Government weather balloon as all electricity was cut by the President. The video made its way to an online video website, *your-television-online.com*. Such distractions alienated the media who were covering the riots in Cairo.

One media reporter covering the riots was an American woman, Tatiana Turan, was raped by Egyptian men as she was not covered up in traditional clothing. Americans cannot go to a foreign country and not obey social customs; it is for their protection. She works for the popular media channel, Roosevelt 180. People who watch that show often do a 180 when they see what is covered.

I asked Bast what she was trying to do in *Tahrir Square* during the previous week. She sat on the poolside resin bench on board the *Athena*, and looked at me strangely, then replied. The *Athena* was still docked at Giza.

"You moderns amaze me. You trade with paper money, a medium with no inherent value, then your governments rack up debt until you cannot spend any more of it. Then you pray for a savior, and a politician comes around who fixes the debt situation so he will be remembered forever. But the politician is voted out of office, another one takes his place and decides to rack up some debt by borrowing from the future, even if a surplus is not there, just an imagined one. This debt is borrowed paper money. It's like this: I have a piece of paper, it has no value until I autograph it, then I exchange it for 100 of your paper notes, or a new chariot. It is still paper. It's a paper-for-paper exchange. Why does paper, or any token, have value? Your Government says this paper note has value, or fiat value. Well, I am a Goddess. My paper money is more valuable than your dead Presidents'. Now what do you think of that?" Bast argued.

I was taken aback by her comments. "Yes... but about Cairo," I said.

"The President of Egypt was a military dictator, who had emergency laws set in place when they were no longer needed. It is like *Julius Caesar* in charge of Rome, forever. When the Senate tired of him, they killed him. More likely, they asked him when he was going to retire? In a few months, he told them. They asked again in a few months, and he said "Consul for Life," then they killed him - no conspiracy there. Same here, the people tired of their dictator so they are removing him from office with this Revolution *I started* as you slept. I apologize for the temporary coma, but I didn't want you to interfere once I suspected *Isfet* was coming," Bast said at length.

"I should probably block the *History Channel* from our satellite dish," I replied.

"Oh don't bother... Much of this is new to me. Your Servant was very informative with the online encyclopedia I found while using the Translation Belt Lady Julia designed," Bast replied.

"I should probably check its batteries," I said. I approached her suddenly, and she turned towards me with one hand in a clawing grasp.

"You forget: you awoke the Goddess in me when you read the *Emerald Scarab* inscription. A *Priestess of Bast* becomes her for about 10 minutes. Power is not something one can be comfortable with all day long. Even Gods sleep." Bast returned to her seat.

"I will keep that in mind," I replied.

Then after a few minutes of relaxing at poolside, Ahmed calls my universal cell phone.

"They did WHAT?!" I demanded. "Oh, so you're just going to let them keep it? Uh-huh, right. Sure, I'll tell her."

"What was that all about?" Bast inquired.

"There was a break-in in the Cairo Museum last night. Thieves stole the *Emerald Scarab*, and are ransoming it for $300,000,000 Egyptian Pounds. It's part of the Revolution's way of earning capital funds. I told him we will see to its return," I said in anger.

Bast stood up with her fists at her side. "I'll meet you there," She told me. "*I call upon the Guardians of Air, Storm and Sea! Come, bring me whence to my destination!*" Dust started to circle at her ankles, and then enveloped her body like a small tornado. The sky's otherwise cloudless sky-scape bellowed with storm clouds from nowhere. She lifted into the air, with lightning shooting from her fingernails. Then her body sailed through the slight breeze, towards Cairo.

I followed her lead via my modified Jet-ski, which was ready to use along one side of my yacht. With my helmet strapped on, and my utility jacket zipped up, I started the engine and drove across the still-moving river. Our Servant would protect the *Athena* from whatever happens.

I noticed Bast was near Gizera Island's Tower, so I switched the engine to Level 2 speed, just enough to reach Cairo without wasting fuel. I was not sure what to expect. There was a large gathering in Central Cairo and a small one near the Khan Bazaar. I parked the Jet-Ski in a discreet location away from prying eyes. Then I continued on foot.

"Halt Thief! I, Bast, Command you!" She ordered the group of thieves as they attempted to sell the *Emerald Scarab* on the Internet.

"Hey! I know you from someplace," said one thief.

"Yeah, you're that woman from *Tahrir Square*! *Viva Revolution*!" said another.

"Return to me the *Emerald Scarab*! Now before I eviscerate your kidneys!" she demanded.

"Oh this?" one thief said. "You will have to fight me for it."

"I wouldn't have it any other way, thief!" Bast said. "*Then* I will eviscerate your kidneys." Bast extended her hands and they became lion claws in seconds.

The thieves exchanged glances as Bast transformed into a lioness and attacked them. One whipped out a blade, so Bast roared at him with her piercing green eyes and sharp incisors. As the thief tried to cut Bast, she released a fireball from her mouth that singed his clothing, compelling him to run away. His accomplice was gathering his laptop and the *Emerald Scarab* before he took off in the opposite direction. Then Bast saw him leave.

"I call upon the animals of the forest! Come, I summon you to my aide," Bast said as she returned to human form. Numerous birds like owls, hawks, and sea-gulls, with domestic cats came by from hiding in car ports and towering buildings and into her presence. She pointed at the thief and the animals complied with her commands. The thief saw this and yelled in horror. Then Bast ran towards him, changing into a leopard. She pounced onto his back and ripped his jacket off. As the thief struggled, she transformed back into the Priestess.

"Who - *What* are you?" he asked in bewilderment. Then she kicked him in his head with her foot, and replied.

"I am Bast. *Hear me Roar*!" she said.

Finding the *Emerald Scarab* on the ground a short distance away, I returned it to Bast who smiled at me.

"Thank you, Doctor," Bast said happily.

The remaining group witnessed this event and gathered around. Some of the elder Muslim population started to kneel and pray towards her, but it was *unclear* if this was worship for her or prayer hour. Others stared in her direction and some started handling their Coptic crosses while chanting.

"Bast, now is not the time for religious devotion," I told her.

"Why? My Egypt *loved* the gods," she said.

"Well, today's Egypt is different. People are not well-versed in religions older than Moses," I told her politely. "They view you as a *pagan* god, something to forget."

"Hahaha! I don't worship trees!" Bast said. "I only worship the *spirit in the trees,* who gives me strength. Pagan? Me? I see the same stories only with different names or faces. I am no more *pagan* than your Coptic *girlfriend.*"

The gathering increased in size. One woman came forth asking for Bast's autograph. Another wanted to take photos with her. Soon the Revolution's main group became interested in Bast. This stopped when the electricity was turned back on, as an apparent diversion from hidden cameras.

Once the electricity was restored, a breaking-news caption was running along the bottom register on Arabic television, in English. Israel had just bombed a site in Northern Iran, near the alleged location of Psamtik's factory. Their reason was that Iran was developing *nuclear weapons.* The only problem was that Israel was in this case correct, just not at that location.

"You have got to be kidding me," I said to Ahmed on my cell phone as Bast and I rode my Jet-ski back to the Yacht. "They didn't even say 'we're sorry, we bombed your food factory and not your weapons stash,' has got to be the worst excuse I've heard from a politician."

"Doctor Costa? What's a nuke?" Bast asked me while piggy-back riding my Jet-ski.

I took time-out from the cell phone to explain a modern weapon used for blackmailing non-industrial nations. “It’s like a fiery ball of explosive heat, like the *Eye of Ra* in the Celestial Cow book,” I informed her.

“But... I **am** the *Eye of Ra*,” She smiled.

“Ra has many eyes,” I replied. “We are thankful to only see two.”

Moments after reaching Giza, air raid sirens started to sound.

“What is that awful noise?” Bast asked.

“Israel,” I started. “They must be under attack by the Iranians.”

In the distance, towards Sinai Peninsula, we saw puffs of colored smoke and sounds of explosions. They did **not** sound like fireworks. I urged Bast to go on board the *Athena* and find some gas masks. Our Servant would help her with that. Arabic television showed the people of Cairo in a panic; some went to bomb shelters while others stormed the *Presidential Palace* for safety. For unclear reasons, the Egyptian President’s private helicopter was seen leaving the building. Some in the crowd cheered as if he abdicated. Then they watched it fly away from Cairo as missiles were witnessed in the distance, flying towards the city. Apparently Iran was not good with artillery.

"We must find shelter!" Julia announced on the forward deck. "Doctor Costa, thank the gods you are okay. Where should we go?"

"The Pyramids seem the best choice," I said. "They were built to withstand the elements. Where is Ahmed?"

"He called. He said he's on his way," Julia said. "This doesn't look good for us. I just wanted to say, if we ever return home, that... You're a good friend."

Ahmed's *Mercedes* car honked its horn as Julia was becoming sentimental. I kissed her forehead and placed an Israeli-made gas mask over her shoulders. Ahmed's car honked again. I escorted Julia off the *Athena*, and locked its doors.

"It's about time you showed up. Where is Omar al-Masri and the others?" I asked Ahmed.

"They are taking shelter in Bast's tomb structure. Yes, I know what you are thinking - that place is eroding, but it's the best below level area we could find on short notice. There is something else. We discovered something after Bast's crypt. Its, an army of some kind, here are the initial photos," Ahmed said.

Ahmed showed me a large cache of giant Shabtis found in the underground structure surrounding Bast's crypt. They all had one thing in common. They all had emeralds on their crest, the same as the *Emerald Scarab*.

"What an expensive find!" I said excitedly. I looked at Ahmed. He wasn't happy with it. "What?"

"Your new friend is not telling us everything. I believe she is using us to find Psamtik and conquer the world with her Shabtis. Psamtik is an excuse, real or not," Ahmed explained.

"I saw her in action... She is on *our* side," I replied.

"Or we are on *her* side. In any event, we must not trust her too deeply. I have reservations about this one," Ahmed said.

"Are you coming?" asked Bast on her way to the Plateau.

"Just trust me," I said to Ahmed.

"I do. Can you *not* trust your gut?" Ahmed said.

I looked into Ahmed's eyes, then at Bast. I thought a moment.

"We're coming!" I announced to Bast.

Ahmed and I ran towards the Plateau and into the Pyramid of Khufu (Cheops), sealing the heavy iron door on our way into the tomb. The air circulation system was operable, thankfully. Julia brought in an ice chest with food and drink rations from the *Athena*. Our servant unrolled a polymesh sleeping bag onto the wooden floor supports. The Pyramid was recently renovated with modern architecture internally to support tourists.

"Hmm.... The television works," Ahmed noticed. "It's good for analog."

For the next several hours, we huddled inside the King's Chamber and lower rooms to the sound of large booming noises outside. One of which felt close by. The Pyramid's internal structure came equipped with flushable latrines, air conditioning, electricity from an external solar panel, and a radio. There were padded cushions inside the Burial Chamber for a *New Age* group that has since left the area. We abided our time reading my collection of self-published novels and Egyptology cook-books. My cell phone reception was mostly static interference via the inclusion of stone blocks.

A day passed by. Julia was worried about the *Athena*, our Servant was tidying up the tomb as he usually does, and Ahmed was studying the blueprints we found in the briefcase via his cell phone camera.

Ahmed asked, "Okay, now what? It's been over a day and the sounds outside have stopped... Do we go outside or continue to wait in here?"

"I should go," Bast replied. "I am a Goddess. I won't be as affected by the radiation. You guys can wait in here."

"You know, she's probably right," Julia said. "She can go out there and tell us when it's safe."

With that, Bast exited the iron gate and sealed it on her departure. Ahmed looked at me and then Julia. I grinned slightly, then took out my Geiger counter and placed it near the gate.

February 6, 2011

Giza Plateau, Giza, Egypt

Inside the Pyramid of Khufu,

1:37pm

One week passed, one agonizing week of waiting. Julia tired of the card games, the Egyptology quizzes that we now know all the answers to, and the games of *Senet*. Our Servant was loyal, and he never complained until the battery died today. We just *had* to go out. No more microwaved, *Ready-to-Eat* Military rations. Our water supply was adequate, except for showering. We reverted to using sponges soaked in soapy water. It is nice how *Aswan Red Granite* absorbs bath water.

I was the first to exit this tomb. The sunlight was strong, the first I felt against my skin in days. . . As I adjusted to the light, I believed I was no longer in Egypt based on what I then saw. At least, it was not *Modern Egypt*. Bast had been busy.

The horizon was different. Scents of flowering gardens replaced the slum of Cairo to the north. Fountains and waterfalls shot up from the landscape as new limestone buildings vied for my attention, in the shape of new Pharaonic temples, palaces, and faience-glazed apartments. Statues carved by non-human hands guarded clean-cut sandstone pylons and polished brass gates. The ground was clean, for once. Nothing so much as a rabid ant dared cross it. Pillars of lotus and papyrus clusters supported solid silver and golden ceilings, with painted star constellations on the underside.

"Whoa," the word escaped my lips in astonishment. This architecture was not just here, but everywhere along the Nile from Giza to Aswan. Cairo was still, well, a slum - *a buried slum*. The sands covered it from a recent, cleansing sandstorm. The people were in hiding, unbeknown to this vision.

There were no cars, and thus no pollution to clean up. The vehicles of this new age were watercraft. Some were Felucca. Others were - hmm, where was the *Athena*?

"Bast? Doctor?" asked Julia on her exit.

"Over here," I said with my back to her, and binoculars in my hands.

"I don't see --," she stopped. "Wow!"

"Doctor Costa, I still don't see how this goddess can possibly," Ahmed stopped. "Oh."

We gazed upon a New Egypt, a *New Kemt*, one that was carefully crafted by a true devotee of the traditional ways.

"Hmm... Instant country - just add people," I said.

"Look! Down there, those walking statues!" Ahmed pointed. "Those aren't.."

"A Shabty Army?" I asked.

A whirlwind appeared before us; then it materialized into a golden-skinned Bast. She was smiling broadly.

"This is *my Egypt*. Enjoy it while it lasts, as I have," Bast said.

Our Servant was the last to exit. He opened his mouth in astonishment, then took out his camera and started photographing everything.

"My Shabtis are not an '*Army*'. Who told you that *delusion*?" Bast warned.

"Actually, I take credit for that," Ahmed replied.

"Then, you're *delusional*," Bast stated as she drifted away.

"Who told you that you could just change Egypt and make it better?" Julia asked Bast.

"I saw destruction, and I felt creation. My Father, Ra, told me once. Go complain to Him, up there in the sky," Bast remarked.

"Was this your plan all along?" Ahmed interjected. "You're *not* going to *conquer* the world?"

"How typical of a male," Bast said. "You presume that because I have power that I am going to abuse my office and destroy civilization. My Divine Parents would *never* approve of that."

"What of Psamtik?" I asked Bast.

"When he comes, we will see," She replied.

"I suppose now you want us to *worship* you?" Ahmed asked.

Bast smiled slightly in acknowledgement. "What you now perceive as Science, We Kemtites perceived as Religion, but in story form."

"There is some truth to that," Julia interrupted. "The Sciences, like Astronomy and basic Physics occur in solar cults. Just look at Akhenaton - true he was a visionary, but he also perceived the Sun as a physical instrument. When the Sun evaporated his offerings, he said *Aton drank them*, so what did he do? He built an open-ceiling temple to see how often the Sun evaporated liquids. To him perhaps it was miraculous, but to us it was the *birth of Science*."

"Like in Mathematics, or Story-problems?" Ahmed asked.

"Exactly," Julia continued. "The ancients created stories or myths to explain their environment. This was scientific observations preserved in popular beliefs. The Temples are like horizons, sending light from the entrance and into the inner sanctum - but only at certain times of the year, like the Solstices. It took great scientific knowledge to know how to build those temples, or Astronomical Observatories."

"And Mother Nature is Science's word for God?" I asked. "As in Natural Selection? You know, the survival of the fittest?"

"I am more fit than Psamtik. Let him come," Bast said.

"Umm.... You're Powerfulness, let us examine your works. I want to learn more of how Ancient Egyptians lived," I said to Bast.

Bast smiled in approval. Bast led me down into the city, and she showed me wonders I never dreamt possible. This city was an anachronistic event, a world from another time and place. The only flaw was there were no people here, only Shabtis. It is people who cultivate civilization, not artifacts. It would just as well be an open-face museum or replica.

Bast showed me the Nilometer, a measuring device to control the level of the river for farming.

She demonstrated how to cultivate grain and scatter it in the air, separating the wheat from the chaff. She showed how to make wine from figs, beer from honey and barley, and bake Faience glass paste with molds for mass production of amulets. The walls of apartments were covered in flat, faience tiles for color and had air circulation in between the walls via a vent in the ceiling called an air-catcher. Faience beads were made by rolling grass in the glass paste, and then fired up in a kiln for stringing. Death masks were crafted from a plaster-like mold of the deceased, then pressed into molten gold and hammered. Most items found in tombs were the best quality items produced by the ancients, except for the fact they were only meant for the afterlife and not used in life. Bast's new city was meant for the living only. This only meant one answer: *The Revolution.*

We remained in this new city for one glorious, no, make that two exciting weeks. We video-graphed it after finding the *Athena* washed up on the western shore of *Philae Island.* Hot showers with real shampoo never felt so cleansing. Bat droppings, aside. Our videos we produced in the production studio for safe-keeping. The people of Cairo were not dead, they still remained in seclusion. Some of them probably were hunting grotto rats or trading pieces of post-government silver in place of *Egyptian Pounds.* If they had popped up to the surface, they would have the opinion they had died and went to *Paradise.*

Towards the end of the last week, an unusually dark cloud appeared near Tanis in the Delta, coming from the East. On closer inspection (with my binoculars) I could see unmanned drones and transport helicopters. They had Persian markings with Late Period glyphs in red ink. It was Psamtik.

I alerted the others. Omar and the remaining group joined us a week ago. Now we were ready. I took out a copy of my old blueprints of the Robot Army specs, searching for a weakness I may have otherwise overlooked. Ahmed was in the Captain's Bridge on the *Athena.* We had gun turrets installed with anti-ballistic missiles. But we had a limited supply. That's where Bast comes in. She controlled her Shabtis, some of which were excellent soldiers once programmed. The *Emerald Scarab* was a thought-sensitive device.

Once Psamtik arrived in full battle formation, as was customary 2200+ years ago, Bast was allowed to greet him, one-on-one, face to face. Psamtik was inside a titanium orb for a head, stuck into a muscular-looking titanium shell of a man, with spears the size of pole-arms. There was my lack of titanium spare parts. He spoke through a translator that buzzed with static.

"BAST! I implore you, remove this scum from the field of battle! It is most unbecoming of us divines," Psamtik said.

"Psamtik! Is it really you? An Immortal? Why the façade? Why the armor?" Bast asked.

"I...I found a new home, a new mission, a new... Conquest. This form you see me in is *temporary*, a necessary shell," Psamtik explained.

"What happened to you? All of *Kemt* wonders!" Bast said.

"Bast, I made an error... I ate the nectar of the Gods, became one of them, saw my family, my friends... I was all alone, the madness of loneliness! So I conquered the Nine Bows, again and again. It was not enough! I craved the world. I wanted to last forever, build monuments all over the Earth.... Power, you see? I am Power incarnate. I can do anything, be anywhere, *Conquer Everyone*!!" Psamtik said in between static interference.

"Look around us," Bast said. "This is Egypt, *Our Egypt*, remember?"

Psamtik examined his surroundings. He winced. "Nothing! This is a replica, a facsimile of *your* making. You did this to trick me into surrendering. Well, stand your ground, and fight me!" Psamtik demanded.

Bast slapped Psamtik on his metal face. Psamtik smirked through his titanium skull, and withdrew into the sky on small jets attached to his legs.

"Let the Battle *Commence*!" Psamtik ordered.

Ahmed fired the *Athena's* gun turrets at the unmanned drones. Other drones attacked the ground. I hopped on my Jet-Ski and opened up the front lights, where small portals opened that revealed laser-guided munitions. Psamtik's army landed, marched towards us and assembled into geometric formations. I pressed a button on my console pad. A speaker with a projection unit opened on top of the *Athena*, and blasted the titanium army with *Tchaikovsky* classical music. The one structural weakness I gleaned from the blueprints was noise friction on the areas where the necks attach to the shoulders. It also sounded nice.

Psamtik swung an electrical rod at Bast before she could react. She fell on the ground and turned into a leopard, then licked her wounds until she was healed. Then she looked up at Psamtik and hissed loudly.

Meanwhile a large flock of Egyptian geese heard Bast's hiss and headed into the fray. As Psamtik raised his right metallic arm, the geese flew into him. Then as Psamtik was busy with the geese, I directed the sound cannon on my yacht into his direction. This caused his Orb to disconnect (his head fell off). Most of Bast's Shabtis were dismembered or otherwise reduced to Alabaster dust, as they were unarmed. Some did manage to take control of some drones and land-based vehicles.

Bast transformed back into the Priestess form, and stood her right foot on Psamtik's Orb. Psamtik then started to laugh uncontrollably.

"You Fool! I am not mortal! I call upon the Storm god *Apophis* to destroy your pitiful legions!" Psamtik dared.

"Your one weakness you never told me was the most obvious one," Bast said.

"Oh? What weakness?" Psamtik demanded while chuckling.

"It is your *Secret Name*!" Bast replied.

"WHAT? I don't *have* a Secret Name!" Psamtik revealed.

"Is it not Psosis?" Bast asked.

"No! My secrets are unknown," Psamtik gloated.

"Then what would it be?" Bast wondered. "Ahh, yes of course! Why didn't I remember it faster?"

"What?"Psamtik asked.

Bast handled the *Emerald Scarab* in her hands while she spoke. "May you enter this trap, O **Kitmasp**! May you enter it forever, you who call yourself **Psamtik**!"

"What? Can't be! NOOO!" Psamtik screamed as his essence exited the Orb and was sucked into the *Emerald Scarab* within seconds. Then all his drones and metallic army stopped abruptly and fell over onto the ground. The battle was over.

Ten minutes passed. We looked over the battlefield, the lifeless Shabtis, the wrecked carnage of pressed titanium. Then as we gathered over the Orb of Psamtik, I saw people. There were lots of people. They came from Cairo, Giza, and beyond our City's pylons and gates. One of them approached Bast.

"We are Egyptians. I don't know what part of Egypt you are all from, but this was my city... We want you as our leader. If it is all the same to you, we love what you've done for Egypt," the man said.

A woman said, "Hail Bast, *the Cat Goddess*!" A cheer of approval came from onlookers and formed a small crowd around the main temple.

Bast looked upon the people and smiled. Our adopted Cat brushed up against Bast's left calf muscle and meowed.

Months later, the Revolution in Egypt had ended. They have found a new Government. Maybe it was not quite what they were expecting. It wasn't entirely a Democracy nor an Islamic State, but a go-between one mixed with history, *their history*. It was a proud history and a new future.

Seven thousand years did not just evaporate, nor did it dissolve into power-crazed dictatorships or corrupt human governments.

Epilogue:

March 11, 2012

Cairo, Egypt

The *Athena* was repaired and eventually made into a tourist ferry. Ahmed became President of the SCA, and found time to excavate the Saqqaran Catacombs as nuclear weapons were no longer seen as powerful compared to the might of a goddess. Bast ruled as *Queen of the People*, a social ruler. She built, using her remaining Shabtis, a huge palace in the desert overlooking Giza. Citizens made offerings to her out of respect, not adoration. Though the *Revolution* existed elsewhere, the one here was appeased. Not everyone has a local deity to look upon. The economy in Egypt was based on education and Science, just as it was long ago...

Julia and I later married. We live in a suburb south of Los Angeles, CA. Our Servant won an award for *Expert Chef* in a local restaurant competition. Omar al-Masri and his group now operate a set of Museums and own a local Café in Alexandria, Egypt. The former President of Egypt suffered a heart attack, but died after seeing the new Egypt blossom like a reborn flower. Iran and Israel signed a peace treaty, because they both feared a desert lion god would obliterate them if they refused.

What of Psamtik and the *Emerald Scarab*? The *Emerald Scarab* was sold to a research foundation with the *Department of Defense* in Washington D.C. It is strongly doubted if it will see the light of day again. The proceeds were spent on a new yacht, dubbed the *Lioness*. Her maiden voyage is set for October, for the waters of Asia...

About the Author:

Michael J. Costa (*not the character*) is an author of over 80 books, and was inspired by Ancient Egypt at a typically young age. He lives in the East Bay Area in Northern California, USA. Michael likes computer games, Egyptian art and culture, with emphasis on replicating some areas in modern times.

Made in the USA
Middletown, DE
13 May 2022